Rosemary

&

Antonio

Rosemary & Antonio   Marie Fostino

This is a work of fiction. All of the characters,
organizations, and events portrayed in this novel are either
products of the author's imagination or are used fictitiously.

ISBN- 13: 978-0692647257

Printed in the United States of America

Chapter One

A Day Unlike Any Other

The alarm went off on the frigid morning of February 14, 1929 – St Valentine's Day. Rosemary eagerly arose and headed to the bathroom to fill the tub. Noticing the time, she knew she had only two hours before she would meet him. She eyed the suitcase open on the chair next to the bed that was filled with her clothes.

The bubbles in her bath were inviting as she climbed in and daydreamed about the coming events of her day. She bathed quickly, her mind racing as she reviewed all the details of their plan. She put on her slip before carefully pinning her long wavy black hair into a French twist. She glanced at herself in the mirror and her reflection cast spitting image of her mothers' large, deep set brown eyes with curly long lashes, and a long wide Italian nose. She put lipstick on her full lips and blush on her cheeks, before donning her off-white skirt, light blue blouse, and matching off-white suit jacket. She glanced at herself and nodded in approval.

Years of memories filled her mind, such as when her mother helped her make the colorful quilt on her bed. Walking past the bed her hand slid across the fabric for the last time. She proudly gazed at the curtains knowing that she had sewn them herself. She remembered how proud her mother was as she was sewing them and asking for help here and there, but not letting her mother touch the sewing machine. Gazing at her dresser with the lace tablecloth, she noticed a picture of her with her parents. She had almost forgotten it. As her hand reached for the frame, she glanced in the mirror to notice she was not smiling. *Why no smile?* She wondered. *Was it all the memories that made her hesitant?*

Nobody would understand the courage it took for her to make this decision. She couldn't stand living in this dangerous town anymore. She wanted a better life than this. But at the same time, the cost would be bigger than she had expected.   She opened her suitcase and delicately folded cloth around the frame so the glass would not break. To the right of her bed was a plaque with ribbons that she had won for spelling tests she had been in throughout the years. Reminiscing about her past almost gave her second thoughts. Her mind was screaming not to go. The quizziness began as she clasped and twisted her hands. Closing her eyes, she took in a deep breath. She didn't want to break anyone's heart, but she also knew she could not stay and longed to be with him. *Would her parents ever forgive her?* Her mind tugged back and forth between her comfort zone and the unknown.

No, she thought, *I want this.*

Grabbing her suitcase, she scanned her room one last time and before she fled down the stairs of her childhood home for the last time. When she stepped outside, a gray sky with a few clouds covered the city. The wind was swift moving and chilled her bones. The branches of leafless trees swayed back and forth keeping the same beat as the hanging traffic lights. A gust of wind swooshed past her shoulders and she shivered. Grabbing a cab was an inviting idea so she could warm herself up. She finally flagged a taxi. Thankfully, the driver got out to fetch her suitcase.

"2100 North Clark Street," she said as the taxi pulled away. Sneaking one last look at the old neighborhood, she sighed.

"Cold isn't it, ma'am," the driver politely asked as he peaked at her through the rear-view mirror.

His kind voice distracted her reverie for a moment, and she thoughtfully nodded before returning her gaze to the world beyond the cab window.

A small smile formed on the driver's lips, but nothing more was said. The streets seemed unusually quiet as they rode to her destination, or was it her imagination due to sneaking off like this.

"Happy Valentine's Day," the driver finally said.

Rosemary raised her chin and displayed a big smile.

"Thank you!" She replied with a giggle as she fantasized about the coming events of the day.

"Someone as pretty as you must have a boyfriend," he continued, "and no doubt will be surprised with flowers."

She could feel her cheeks deepen to the shade of crimson. As if keeping out the cold, she hugged herself. He glanced back at her for a moment and smirked, a small laugh leaving his throat. A little uncomfortable, she cleared hers.

"And who are you buying flowers for today?" She asked nervously, her fingers rubbing her arms. *Did he know who she was and where she was going?* Her mind now anxious with fear wished she was not in this cab with this man who seemed to know more than what he was saying.

She was careful not to say a word to anyone about who she was involved with. She knew the kind of trouble she would be in if a certain couple of people found out about them. She grew weary on the man driving while waiting for his answer. *Was he on the payroll to keep an eye on her?* She thought back to their plans and could not remember telling anyone what they were going to do. Maybe she was just being paranoid. Strange things have happened since she met Antonio.

"It better be my wife," he snickered. That answer relaxed her and she let her arms fall to her lap. *How could he know, she was just being silly, although, you can never be too careful?*

"What color roses does she favor?" Rosemary asked to keep the conversation going. She didn't want him to notice her fright. Her eyes never left him. She watched him shake his head as he thought.

"Mm, I think pink." He speculated. "Good idea! I had better get pink ones. Thanks!" With his eyes still on the road he asked, "And what is your favorite color young lady?"

"I would be happy with any color," she quickly responded before twisting her head toward the side window to her right. The suspicion left her mind as she went back to her fantasy of the adventure that awaited her.

They rode the rest of the way to her destination in silence. Her mind filled with thoughts of Antonio. He made her pulse rise with excitement. No one had ever made her feel like that before.

When they arrived, the taxi driver retrieved her suitcase from the trunk while she exited the vehicle. A few snowflakes started to fall bringing back memories of the first time she met Antonio.

"Thank you, and don't forget the pink roses for your wife," she said with a smile as she paid him.

He smirked and gave her a quick nod before returning to his cab. Rosemary strolled to a nearby coffee shop and chose a table where she could sit and relax. Memories of the first time they met entered her mind; how he had asked to sit with her because there were no more empty tables, how every day after that he would wait for her with a cup of coffee sitting next to him for her. The smell of coffee and sweet jellyrolls filled the air. A few people sat talking or just reading a newspaper. Rosemary checked the delicate watch on her wrist. She still had a little time to kill before Antonio would arrive.

"Can I get you anything?" asked the polite waiter in a crisp white apron. Rosemary glanced up at him with a look of uncertainty.

She closed her eyes and took a deep breath before nodding her head.

"Coffee please."

"Would you like anything else, a sweet roll perhaps?"

"No thanks, coffee's fine."

When he returned with the steaming cup, she thanked him and folded both hands around it before taking a sip. Staring out the front window, she became lost in her thoughts again. The smell of the baked goods made her think about baking pies with her mother, which in turn made her feel homesick. She wondered how bad she was going to hurt the two people that she loved all her life. And of course, there was Al, but she was pretty sure he wouldn't miss her. Why he may even be glad she is gone and out of his life; one less person to protect.

Yet dreaming of Antonio's face made her forget her fears and become anxious for their day to begin. Impatiently, she glanced at her wristwatch again, but little time had passed. It was only half past ten. She picked up her cup and was about to take another sip when she detected the shrill sound of gunfire. Panic stricken, she held her breath. Then she leapt out of her seat and ran to the door. The sound of chairs scraping the floor were all that could be heard as others ran as she did to look outside.

Through the café window she watched the caper go down. From the garage across the street, two men exited with the bull quick on their heels. She tried to focus on them without being noticed. She was not sure if she recognized any of them. All four of them entered a Cadillac sedan and sped away. She did not see blood or any bodies lying on the ground thankfully. Knots formed in the pit of her stomach. She felt like something was wrong. In her heart she knew she had to investigate further. As the car sped away, the loud chatter of different ideas of what may have happened filled the coffee shop. The crowd dispersed back to their seats.

Rosemary left her chilled coffee on the café table with a small tip and exited. No sooner than she let the door slip someone wearing a tan overcoat and hat bumped into her. She heard whoever he was mumble an apology before he disappeared inside. She hesitated for just a small moment; with the idea she knew who this man was. She felt an uncomfortable sensation run through her body when he bumped into her. *Maybe she recognized him? Could that be Bugs?* But the fleeting thought left her just as fast as she ran toward the garage. Fighting the wind took her breath away and sent a new chill through her body. When she reached the door, she hesitated for a moment before touching the knob. It seemed like slow motion as she turned her hand and opened the door. She waited for only a moment to listen, but the only sound was her footsteps as she stepped with one foot deliberately in front of the other past the offices at the front of the building. Taking a deep breath first, she reluctantly opened the door to the garage. It made an eerie creaking sound as it exposed what was behind it. Without warning, a gasp escaped her lips as she stumbled upon a horrible scene. Her hand slapped across her mouth trying to contain any kind of fear she may let out. She had heard stories about things like this, but she could never have imagined them happening in real life.

Tears filled her eyes as she tried to focus on the bloody sight before her. The brick wall was sprayed red. Blood slowly dripped to the floor where seven men lay dead; their bodies riddled with bullet holes. She stood memorized by the horrific sight in front of her. Then fear took over her body and she stiffened, afraid to move. Hearing tales of such violence was incomparable. Standing there it seemed as if the blood was slowly seeping toward the door. Was she hallucinating? One of the bodies attempted to crawl to the door through the bloody mess. He stopped and squinted up at her before he called her by name.

"Rosemary... get out of here... now," he labored to say in his weakened state.

Chapter Two

A Year Earlier: February 1928

"Come and help me in the kitchen, Rosemary," shouted her mother. "You do want to catch a husband someday, don't you?"

Rosemary lagged a little longer in her room before she finally made her way down the stairs to the kitchen. Her nose filled with the delicious seasonings of pasta sauce boiling on the stove. The table was covered with flour, eggs, oil and water as mom mixed the ingredients together to make ravioli noodles.

Her mother, Darlene, was a full blood Italian woman. She had a small face with big cheeks, and lots of black and white hair that she always pinned up on her head. She was well endowed with the years of birth and good food which reflected in her wide hips. Her father said that one of the reasons he married her was for her terrific cooking skills.

"Hi, Mama," Rosemary said entering the kitchen.

The kitchen was small with enough room for a table to work on and four chairs. The cabinets with glass doors, showing the white dishes stacked neatly in place and the matching cups hanging from hooks. The floor was checker board black and white tile. The sink was mounted to the wall with attached drain boards and two legs.

Her mother gave her a kiss on the head as she passed her an apron. Darlene's hands were covered with flour from balling up and kneading the dough until it was well mixed.

"How are you ever going to learn how to cook, if you don't spend time in the kitchen?" She asked.

Rosemary rolled her eyes. She was the first person in her family to obtain a high school diploma. She knew her parents were proud of her succeeding at something they had no opportunity to acquire. Her mother grew up helping her grandmother at home cooking, cleaning, and assisting with the care of her siblings. To her mother, a woman's place was in the home, but Rosemary had always dreamed of more.

"I'm studying, Ma," she answered quickly as she dusted the table with more flour.

"Don't you want me to be something when I get out of school?" she asked with some annoyance. "I had to finish my English homework."

"You are something, child," mom replied with a laugh. Her strong New York accent dropping the R she still had even after all this time living in Chicago. "And there is more to life than school. You need a husband someday. The only way to a good man's heart is through his stomach." She handed Rosemary a rolling pin and they both rolled out the dough for the noodles. Fortunately, Rosemary did know how to cook. Her mother brought her up to help out in the kitchen. Together they cooked meals often. She admired the love her mother put into her cooking and wished she felt the same, but something was missing. She didn't know what it was, but she wanted more for herself than to be a housewife.

"I thought I might want to be a teacher, Ma," Rosemary continued as she worked. "I'm not sure I want to get married yet." She has had this conversation before and it always ends up the same way. Men work and woman stay home to cook and have babies. She could not get her mother to understand, this was the 1920's and things were changing for women. Why women could now vote and hold down jobs. They didn't have to stay home anymore if they didn't want to.

Her mother shook her head and chose to ignore her remarks.

"I married your father when I was 18, child. That's what life is all about – getting married, having babies, and making good pasta." She paused from rolling the dough for a moment to glance up at her daughter before adding, "All decent Italian women are married young and start a family."

"Well, how did I do?" Asked Rosemary. She also decided to overlook her mother's comments but never stopped working with the flour on the table.

She set down her rolling pin and looked for the ravioli filling. Her mother touched the dough with the palm of her hand. She seemed to know by the feel, if it was too thick or too thin. She nodded her approval as Rosemary opened the refrigerator to take out a bowl of ricotta cheese and sausage.

"You did well, child," she said passing a spoon to Rosemary. "Keep this up and you'll find a husband soon." They took the filling and spooned it onto the rolled-out dough.

"So who's coming for dinner tonight, Ma?" Rosemary inquired. It was the Italian way to have a friend or two over to eat.

She smoothed the filling with a spoon pushing it to the sides of the pasta. Then she followed her mother's actions as she took a knife and cut long lines down the cheese-filled pasta.

"Your father's friends... Al, John, and William Thompson will be here," she replied.

Upon hearing those names, Rosemary scrunched up her nose. These three men were not on her favorite list.

"They give me the creeps, Ma," she noted as she concentrated on making triangles out of the pasta squares and pinching the sides firmly together.

"Rosemary, watch your tongue. They are important men. If it were not for Al, our grocery store could not survive. His men keep us safe from the other hoodlums out there and William . . . is the mayor of Chicago. . . We should be honored that the mayor likes to come here for dinner."

Her mother grabbed a big pot and filled it with water. She placed it on the stove with the lid shut tight to let it boil. Rosemary took a wooden spoon out of the drawer to taste the pasta sauce. This subject was nothing to argue about, so she just went along with the usual routine.

"You outdid yourself again, Ma," she said putting her spoon in for seconds.

"Thank you, dear, now please help me clean off the table."

The water came to a boil and mom placed the little triangles filled with cheese and meat into the pot. Then they quickly cleaned the kitchen and set a large dining table in the downstairs recreation room.

The family home had three floors. The main floor had a kitchen, living room, small dining room, bathroom, and a bedroom. A couple more bedrooms were upstairs, and the basement served as the place where they had their meals with friends and held other types of gatherings.

Rosemary's father, Mike Macino, was watching the news and reading the paper. You could tell by his face with the deep lines under his eyes and his receding hairline that he had aged quite a bit over the years. However, his thick dark eyebrows, Roman nose, and curved chin showed that he was still a good-looking Italian man. He was short; about five foot four and heavy set. His waist seemed to increase with time, undoubtedly due to his wife's good cooking. His accent was even thicker than her mom's. At six o'clock there was a knock at the front door.

"Welcome, Al... John," said Mike as he let his two guests inside.

They were used to coming over and after shaking hands the two guests went straight to the basement stairs. Mike waited upstairs for his third guest to arrive. As they reached the bottom, Darlene rushed by with a platter of ravioli.

"Smells good," said Al and took the platter from her hands.

"Thank you," she replied with a smile.

Al put the plate down and gave Darlene a quick kiss on the lips before she ran back to the stairs. John Torrio then grabbed her and kissed her just as she made her way to the stairs. Darlene started up the stairs as Rosemary walked down with the pasta sauce. She closed her eyes just for a moment and took a deep breath, she knew what was coming up next and she was not looking forward to it. Slowly lowering the bowl onto the table, she noticed out of the corner of her eye that John followed her every move.

"Hey, little lady," he said turning toward her, "Where is my kiss?"

Rosemary smiled and reluctantly obeyed, slowly entering his arms. He grabbed her by the waist and kissed her quickly. She was like a robot – doing what she was told with no feeling.

"Hey, Rosemary," sang Al after John let her go.

Hesitantly, she approached Al. He grabbed her by the waist and kissed her as well. "You need to put on a little weight, girl," he said

16

and smacked her behind as she headed back to the stairs.

With one foot following the other and her hands sliding up the rails, Rosemary quickly ran back up the stairs to her mother while wiping her mouth with the back of her hand. Stomping through the kitchen she grabbed the rolls from the counter and started thrusting them into a basket.

"What's wrong, dear?" Asked her mother.

She bit her lip, wondering if she should say anything. She was told that all Italian men greet the women that way. Kissing was an Italian custom. They didn't intend to disrespect her, only to say hi. Darlene observed her daughter before slowly moving to her side. Putting both hands on her daughter's shoulders, she gave Rosemary a pleading look. All she could do was let out a sigh.

"I hate it when they have to kiss me," she said. In any case it was done, over with, something she had no choice but to endure it. She paused for a moment to see if there was going to be any comment from her mother, but she simply stood listening and waiting.

"They have to put their whole mouth over mine. It's disgusting," she added making a face to show her distain. "I am not a little girl anymore, Ma."

"It's tradition dear," her mother replied in an authoritative voice not seeming to see anything wrong with their actions. She pulled Rosemary in close for a quick hug before gazing into her naïve eyes. "I know you're not a little girl any more. You are a beautiful young lady

17

and I am very proud of you." Her head tilted to the side as a loving smile grew on her lips. "Hurry, we need to get the rest of the food downstairs before it gets cold."

***

Rosemary's father was a quiet man, born in Italy and brought to the states as a young child. He lived in Brooklyn, New York along with his cousin, Al Capone.

Mike never finished school, having quit at age 16 to help his father out in the family store. He spent his days assisting his dad and taking care of customers. That is how it was, family taking care of family, the Italian way.

Meanwhile, Al, his cousin, went in a different direction and eventually down a dangerous path. He was born in Brooklyn, a middle child of a large Italian immigrant family. As early as the age of fourteen his temper got the best of him when he hit his teacher whom he thought was unfairly lecturing him. The pressure of school was hard for him, keeping up with assignments, and being nice when he didn't feel like it. Each day blended into the next, and all anyone was concerned about was his grades and not how he felt. So, he dropped out of school and tried to work a few honest jobs. He worked as a candy store clerk, a bowling alley pin boy, a laborer in am ammunition plant, and a cutter for a book bindery, all the while serving in the South Brooklyn Rippers and Forty Thieves Juniors, bands for delinquent boys known for vandalism and petty crime. By the time he was sixteen years old he became a member of the notorious Five Points gang in Manhattan. He worked for a gangster named Frankie Yale as a bouncer and bartender. In those days a bouncer had to be tactful, someone who could radiate authority while having a silver tongue. Al seemed to be quite good at this. With this role, Al considered himself a protector, not a thug.

While working at the bar one day, a man walked in with his sister and a girlfriend. Al could not keep his eyes off this man's sister. She was a sight to behold. Eventually he worked up the courage and asked her out. When she refused his offer with grace, he walked away. But that didn't stop him from appreciating her beauty from afar. A little later Al attempted to ask her out again. She instantly refused. This time her brother took action. Being a gentleman, he asked the girls to leave before discussing the matter with Al.

As the girls left Al shouted to Lena, "You have a nice ass, honey, and I mean that as a compliment."

Lena's brother demanded an apology on behalf of his sister. Al did not take kindly to being told what to do. As he advanced the man pulled out a knife and was quick to stab Al – twice in the face and once on the neck. Al was rushed to the hospital and received eighty stitches. The scars will forever be a reminder of that day.

Al's first arrest was on a disorderly conduct charge while working for Frankie. As he continued down this road, his conduct became increasing worse. Later Al shot the winner of a neighbor's craps game as he robbed him of his winnings. Al's crimes escalated. He murdered two men without a blink of an eye, though charges were never brought against him.

One night a few years later a gang arrived at Mike's parent's store and ransacked the place, tearing it to shreds. His parents never saw it coming. They tried to fend off the hoodlums, but it was no use. They both died protecting what was theirs. Following the murders, Frankie was concerned for Al. His safety was priority. The hoods must have known that Mike's parents were relatives of Al's. It was one way of getting back at Al. Frankie decided to send Al to Chicago for a while until things cooled down. At Al's pleading, Mike decided to move his family to a Chicago neighborhood as well. Al talked him into the move so he could start a new life with a promise of no strings attached. His guilt made him feel the need to protect Mike and his family. After all, if it wasn't for him, maybe Mike's parents would still be alive. Mike did not approve of what Al did for a living and wanted no part of that life. However, Al helped him obtain a house and start his own local corner store for which he was most grateful. After all, they were family. As time went on, Mike was there whenever Al needed him.

Eventually, Al went to work for John Torrio, Frankie's old mentor. John was the leader of the South Side gang in Chicago and admired Al for both his intelligence and physical strength. They got along so well that

John promoted him to manage his bootlegging business. They eventually became partners in the saloons, gambling houses, and brothels. Everything was going smooth, that is until the North Side gang started to get in the way.

George Moran was known in Chicago as a gangster who was incarcerated three times before turning twenty-one years of age. He was born in St. Paul, Minnesota and while going to a private school, he joined a juvenile gang and left school at the age of eighteen years old. George seemed to have trouble with authority and gang life exploited his need to fit in. After robbing a little store, he was sent to the state juvenile correctional facility. Concrete and bars couldn't contain him any more than the private school could contain his spirit. He escaped, and it wasn't long before he found himself in the middle of another robbery. He fled to Chicago and got caught trying to rob a warehouse, taking part in a horse-stealing ring and taking part in a robbery involving the death of a police officer. Unfortunately, the bull got wacked, and George boy went up state to do hard time for a while. Eventually he joined a North Side gang lead by Dion O'Bannion.

Due to prohibition which banned the distribution of alcohol beverages, resulted in bootlegging. The two gangs fought violently on selling the liquor.

John, who was the leader of the South Side gang, disliked violence and tried to establish rules to prevent future fighting. His plan involved establishing a partnership between himself and Dean. Dean was the head of the North

Side boys. If all went according to plan, they would each have their own side of the city to sell whisky and make money without getting in each other's hair.

However, plans are only as good as the paper they are written on, and the boys had other ideas. A Sicilian group of brothers known as the Gennas were partners with John already. They wanted to extend their interests into other territories. The South Side boys were becoming a huge part of the Chicago area in bootlegging and the money was rolling in. The Gennas were greedy. They willfully ignored the partnership that John tried to create and decided to market their whiskey in the North Side of Chicago – Dion's territory.

Things started to heat up when the Gennas moved their liquor where it didn't belong and sold it for half the price. Naturally, Dion felt he was being cheated on his own turf and went to see John to ask for help. John, still trying to be the peacemaker, tried to talk Dion into some of the South Side brothel proceeds to make up some of the money he lost, but since Dopn was against prostitution he would not accept. John had to put his foot down and managed to talk the Gennas out of what they were doing, but it was too late, the damage was done.

Dion was angry and wanted revenge, so he decided to strike back by hijacking the Gennas' shipments of liquor and then turn around to sell it himself. Whenever he had the chance, he insulted the Italians severely by calling them 'grease balls' and 'dagos.' As his anger got the best of him, he would insult Al using the press by calling him 'scar face'.

The war of words quickly snowballed after two further events between the two, which made Chicago a dangerous place to reside. The first occurred between Dion and the Gennas when he arrived to collect a $30,000 debt that they owed him. Al explained that they could not pay and asked if they could pass it on as good faith to keep the peace, but Dion angrily refused. He later called the Gennas demanding that the debt be repaid within a week.

In the second incident, Dion contacted John and told him he wanted to retire from the business; that, he was interested in selling him some of his profits. John, of course, became overly excited to hear that, and thought of the peace it might create. He met Dion at a warehouse and when they started to talk, the police arrived to arrest both of them for prohibition-related crimes. After all, prohibition was instituted with the enactment of the 18th Amendment, which forbids the distribution of alcoholic beverages. They both posted bail, but when John realized Dion had actually set up the raid, the Italians voted to kill him. That's when all hell broke loose!

Al was a man of many faces. He ate in restaurants with ordinary people around and let himself be seen talking to anyone who said hi to him. To the public, he was sort of a modern-day Robin Hood since he also made donations to many charities. Mike was grateful to his cousin. It was because of him that he could provide a good and normal life for his family.

Also during that time, Al's wheel house was an elaborate ruse. A gambit where he owned every cog, even the mayor of Chicago himself, William Hale Thompson. He was advantageously at ease in an era when death was the way of life.

***

The doorbell rang and Mike quickly answered it to find William holding a bottle of wine.

"Am I late?" He asked as he handed the bottle to Mike.

"You're just in time," he said as they shook hands before he ushered him toward the stairs.

The girls were still upstairs in the kitchen when William made his way down. All four men, including Al and John, shook hands and sat at the table.

"So how was Italy, John?" Asked Al. "We sure missed you."

John squirmed in his seat. His mind went back in time to an unfortunate incident. It was a Saturday afternoon when he was shopping with his wife, Anna. It had been a delightful day. The sun was shining and they were having such a good time. On their return home, however, an unexpected hail of gunfire shattered the glass of the car window hitting his body. The screams of his wife couldn't be heard through the sound of the gunfire. They had just parked the car and before opening the door, the gunfire began.

John lay back in the seat bleeding with bullet holes in his body.

Leading Dion's man, Bugs, walked up to the car, looked him in eyes, and pointed his gun right at him. He saw his wife sitting there shaking but he didn't care. Anna screamed, but as he pulled the trigger, the gun jammed. The rest of Dion's crew yelled at Bugs to get out of there immediately before the police showed up. He hesitated only for a moment, taking in the scene in front of him, hoping he had killed John. He took their advice and bolted. Anna held her husband's body, which was swimming in blood. She screamed again as tears rolled down her face. She held onto her husband and waited for an ambulance to arrive. John survived emergency surgery and recovered slowly.

Al had his men keep an eye on him day and night to keep him safe just in case Bugs tried to pull something like that again. After his release from the hospital, he served a year in jail, but even there he kept the code of silence and never told anyone the identity of his attempted assassins. His near death and prison experience frightened him so much that after his jail time, he moved to Italy with his wife and mother. He quit the mob business completely, a promise he made to his wife, leaving Al in charge.

"I told you before Al, I quit," he said with a big smile. "You don't know what it's like to see your life flash before your eyes." He paused and no one said a word so he continued. "I do... I want to live a little longer with Anna."

"Well, it's good to see you, old friend," Al replied with a sincere smile while patting him on the shoulder. "Glad you still consider me as your friend."

Then his eyes flashed up to William. He already knew where he stood with the Mayor.

"And you Bill, how are things? Am I still in business?"

William sat straight up before he answered. His lips twisted into a wry smile.

"Of course you are! As long as you're in the south side of Chicago." He tilted his head and gave a wink.

Al opened his jacket. William's eyes never strayed. He watched Al's every movement as if his life depended on it. From an inside pocket, he pulled out a wad of money and handed it to the mayor. William took the money graciously, placed it in his pants pocket, and they shook hands.

They could hear the rustle of the girls coming down the stairs.

"Hey guys," said Mike. "No more shop talk."

They all shook their heads in agreement. As the women descended the stairs, the men stood up and waited until they sat down before retaking their seats.

"It sure does smell good," said Bill and placed some ravioli on his plate. He passed the serving dish on to Al. The sound of spoons clinking on platters was a joyful sound to Darlene's ears.

"Darlene is a great cook," Al laughed as he loaded up his plate. As he passed the plate to

Mike, he gave Darlene a nod of approval with a big grin. He knew this would be an excellent meal.

"Thanks for asking me over," John said before taking his first bite. "One thing I've missed since I moved away is your wife's cooking, Mike."

"Come on boys," she blushed. "Flattery will get you nowhere."

The rest of the night was full of homemade food and friendly conversation.

Chapter Three

A Chance Meeting

At 18 years old, Rosemary attended the Chicago Normal College so she could get an education to become a teacher. Her days were occupied with a full load of English, science, geography, chemistry, music, and art. School was an all day ordeal from 9 a.m. to 3 p.m. and failure to keep up with one's classes meant reassignment to a special section. Rosemary's father and mother were born in Italy and came to the United States when they were young. They always told her that America was a place of opportunity. She grew up in a typical Italian household where family members took care of each other. The men worked and the women cared for the children. Rosemary was thankful that she had acquired her high school diploma – something her parents could not do. Her parents were so proud of her, but she wanted more from life and nothing was going to stop her.

She never minded that she had to walk to the bus stop and then stroll several blocks to the college. She had a deep concern for people and wanted to make a difference in the world. Her dream was to one-day help children acquire a good education so they could make something of themselves as well.

It was a pretty winter day in February with the sun shining and the snow glistening on the ground like diamonds. Rosemary donned her coat and scarf before she marched out the door into the frigid air. Her parents had already gone to work at the store. The cold shrill of the wind cut right through her as she began her walk to the bus stop. The bus was not too crowed this morning, so she took a seat and enjoyed her little reprieve from the wind until she got near the school and had to get off. As she walked in the direction to school, she stopped at a coffee shop, like she did every morning, for a hot cup of coffee to warm herself up. While sitting at a table taking a sip, her ears picked up when she heard a musical voice.

"Hello," he said.

She glanced up at his dazzling face with his charming smile. He seemed tall compared to petite stature, since she was only about five foot three. His dark hair was dotted with white specks of snow that had yet to melt.

"Hello," Rosemary said with a curious smile. She was not accustomed to associating with strangers. It was when he pulled up a chair to her table it startled her.

"Do you mind if I sit here with you?" He asked as he glanced around the room shaking his head. "There are no more chairs left and I would like to warm up with some coffee too."

She nodded in the affirmative and he sat down. He raised his hand toward her before he spoke again.

"My name is Antonio May, and you are?"

She took his hand, which seemed clean except around the finger nails, cautiously and shook it. Her eyes glanced at his face before she responded.

"I'm Rosemary Macino." She quickly withdrew her hand and eyes. She placed both hands tightly around her coffee cup curling with her fingers.

"Are you going to school here?" He asked.

She nodded her head again and took a sip of her coffee.

"And you?" She asked as she slowly raised her head.

He paused for a moment and then met her gaze.

"I'm an apprentice at the garage down the street," he replied. "I'm learning to be a mechanic." She did not acknowledge his remark, but her eyes never left his face so he went on. "What are you taking in college?" He asked staring at her with genuine interest. His eyes seemed to penetrate her entire being.

The intensity of his stare caused her to shift nervously in her seat. *Who is this daring man and why does he talk to me like we are old friends,* she thought?

"I'm getting my education to become a teacher," she said and quickly glanced back at her coffee.

Taking one last sip Rosemary swiftly rose from the table, grabbed her coat and scarf, and proceeded to put them on. At the same time, she could not help noticing his raised eyebrows.

"Thank you for sharing your table with me," he smiled.

She offered him a quick smile in return before she retreated out the door back into the cold. Taking one careful step at a time she tried not to slip on the icy sidewalk.

Her encounter of this man lingered in her mind. She carried on to school and the rest of the day continued as usual. She enjoyed her English, Science and Music classes but it was alarming difficult to concentrate. Her mind drifted back to the handsome stranger she had met earlier that day at the coffee shop.

When she walked out of the school at the end of her day, a new layer of snow covered the parking lot and whitened the streets. Snow balls were being thrown and some students were sliding on the icy paths. She had to be extra careful not to slip and fall as she made her way to the bus stop. As she meticulously maneuvered the sleek sidewalk, a car drove up beside her and a friendly voice called out.

"Can I give you a lift home?"

Rosemary continued to walk increasing her speed, as she tried to desperately ignore him but the car slowly rolled along beside her. She kept her eyes forward with the intent of not noticing it.

"Please come in and get out of the cold," the magical voice said.

Rosemary was to the point of shivering and had no idea how long she would have to wait for the bus. She pulled the scarf tighter around her neck. The bus was likely to be crowded. Rosemary feared she would be standing sandwiched between other bodies trying not to bump them every time it stopped. One thing she did know was that given the weather, it would likely be late. She fought in her mind; she really did not talk to strangers, yet the idea of standing outside was definitely not a welcome one. If he was going to hurt her, he would have done it already. As Al's cousin she was taught to be careful. Trust was to be earned, not given freely. Finally, she convinced herself that he was not really a stranger. After all, she met him that morning in the coffee shop.

The moment she made up her mind to trust him, she stopped dead in her tracks. Antonio was quick to pull over and jump out of the car. As she approached the vehicle, he opened the passenger door for her.

"Where to, madam," he said with a chuckle before he shut her door and slid back to his side of the car.

After Antonio got back into the car Rosemary nonchalantly gave him her address. Her heart leapt wildly in her chest. Her hands gripped her school books tightly on her lap. She nervously tucked a stray hair behind her ear. She instantly regretted getting inside.

"So how was school today?" Antonio asked trying to break the silence.

"Fine," she replied with one simple word, avoiding conversation.

"Well I had a good day cleaning out carburetors," the soft voice said. She bit her lip, but didn't answer. An uncomfortable silence blanketed the car.

The streets were slippery and Antonio kept his eyes peeled on the road. Rosemary was intensely aware of him sitting close enough to touch yet distant. Even though she looked straight ahead, out of her peripheral vision she could see this man with a steady hand concentrate on his driving to bring her home safely. About a block before they reached her house, she asked him to stop. She was not sure how her parents would feel about a strange boy driving her home. Not understanding, he nevertheless followed her wishes and pulled over. Then he jumped out again to get her door for her. She could not believe the rush of emotion that pulsed through her at that moment. *Could he be feeling this too?* She wondered.

"Thank you for the ride," she said sincerely after he helped her out of the car.

Antonio tilted his head in her direction.

"She talks," was all he said in a still, small voice.

Rosemary watched him as he sped away and then carefully walked the block home in the cold.

Chapter Four

Antonio Meets Bugs

Rosemary would later learn that Antonio was 19 years old and born in Chicago. He was one of seven children of John May, an auto mechanic. Once he helped his dad wash the family car when he was a child, his own passion for cars began to grow. Antonio enjoyed watching the different cars that pulled into his father's garage for repairs.

One of John's most valuable customers was George 'Bugs' Moran. Bugs, born to Irish and Polish immigrant parents, grew up on the north side of Chicago. He ran with numerous gangs and was in jail three times before turning the young age of 21. He eventually became a member of Dean's North Side gang. Together, they led the boys with numerous shootouts in which he was a lead player. He was also the gunman who tried to assassinate John.

"Okay, son," Antonio's father said as they stood in his garage with a couple of cars sitting there. He wanted his son to look at the 1928 Ford Sedan. He told the owner it would be finished today.

"Let's see if you've been paying attention and studying like I asked you to do."

He walked around his son with a grin on his face, never letting his eyes leave the boy before he moved toward the Ford and popped open the hood.

"How do you clean a carburetor?" He asked with a sneaky smile.

Antonio cocked his head, glanced at his dad for a couple of seconds and then he checked out the engine. He could feel his dad's eyes on him as he looked under the hood.

"Well, cleaning the carburetor would ensure the desired performance and reliability," Antonio replied with words he memorized from the text book.

He took out the cotton tool roll that held the appropriate wrenches and laid them out on the bench besides him before turning up his sleeves. The steel hit the bench with a loud clatter breaking the silence.

"I have to remove the filter screen."

Antonio leaned over the hood, cranked the wrench, and removed the filter in front of the float bowl. His finger nails were laden with grease and his clothes smelled of exhaust. Then he took off the brass plug at the bottom of the carburetor and drained it. His dad walked closer to the engine making sure that his son knew what he was doing. But just before he could say good job, he noticed his son did not replace the filter right away. He took a turkey baster and attached a clear plastic hose to the end of it. His father, John, watched with amazement at what his son was doing.

"I read that if I use this through the filler cap, I can remove sentiment from the

35

bottom of the gas tank," Antonio noted after he glanced up to see his father's confused face.

John chuckled as he watched his son finish cleaning out the carburetor and put it back together.

"Nicely done, son!" he complimented as Antonio began to clean up. "And where did you read this thing with the turkey baster?" Antonio closed the hood.

Before Antonio had the chance to respond the clomping sound of footsteps echoed throughout the garage. Both men turned their attention toward the noise. John glanced up to see Bugs walking in.

Antonio's eyes grew big as he gazed at three men dressed to the hilt in pin stripped suits and hats. He grabbed a rag and tried to wipe the black soot off his fingers. George Moran walked in with an arrogant stride. The other two men were Peter and Frank Gusenberg, top gunmen of George.

"So how is it going, John?" George asked as he walked up to shake his hand.

John wiped his hand with his handkerchief before extending it.

"Your car is as good as new, Sir. My son is even teaching me a few tricks about cleaning carburetors," he added with a quick wink in Antonio's direction. Antonio quickly brought his shoulders up standing tall and straight. He thought he saw George turn and give him a slight smile before walking to his car.

George walked up to the car and nodded to Peter to open the hood.

"So, you did this, son?" George asked as he placed both hands on the frame of the car and looked down inside the engine. Frank walked around the car inspecting it.

"I I only cleaned the carburetor, Sir," Antonio stuttered excitedly. How proud he felt that his dad worked for important men like this. *They must be important to dress like they did and to own this car,* he thought. "Dad is teaching me to become a mechanic."

Bugs closed the hood and turned to face Antonio.

"Want to hear her run?" Antonio asked running to the driver's side. He jumped into the car and turned the key. The car came to life with a purring sound making everyone turn and look. He hit the gas a couple of times and then let her run for a couple more minutes before turning her off.

"Sounds good doesn't she?" he commented as he got out of the car.

A big smile formed on Bug's face. Then he looked at John to offer a look of satisfaction.

"Your father is a good man, son," he said as he reached into his pocket to pay him. "You're learning from the best."

"Thanks, George," said John as he accepted the money.

"Keep it up son," George said. "Who knows, maybe one day you will be working on my cars." Antonio's mouth got wide with a big smile showing all his teeth.

Bugs lifted his chin with a thankful nod before the men got into the car and drove out of the garage.

"Wow, dad, are those important men?" Antonio inquired with excitement in his voice. "I want to dress and own a car just like them."

John bent down to pick up some tools before he answered him. Antonio followed his lead.

"Let's just say they are powerful men, son," John said as he took a rag and wiped grease off some of the tools. "They are also dangerous men, so be careful around them." He waited for the loud, ringing, metallic sound from inside the tool kit as the wrenches were being tossed back inside to quit before he went on. "Their life is not the kind of life you want to live, son."

"Why?"

"Because that was George 'Bugs' Moran. He is with the North side boys. I don't want any son of mine being mixed up with people like that."

Antonio searched his father's face as he scratched his head, for further explanation, he didn't elaborate.

"Dad, you work for him, don't you?"

A stern voice came out of John which surprised Antonio. "No, son, I don't." His face was taunt and his lips straight. "I work on his car, but I am not part of his gang nor will I ever be."

"I don't understand?"

"What is there to understand? We make a clean living, we fix cars. We don't go out and shoot people when asked, do we?"

Antonio's brow furrowed. His father could see him chewing on more than his bottom lip. He knew he would have to explain more about Mr. Moran and his choice of friends.

"You have read the papers, I assume. You know that we have a couple of gangs here in Chicago that fight over territory. Well, the South Side is led by Al Capone and the North Side is led by George Moran."

"Dad, if this man is as bad as you say, isn't it dangerous for you to be fixing his car?"

John closed his eyes while taking in a deep breath. He knew his son was correct, and he knew he had to give him a good reason. Peering outside of his garage he let his eyes trail down the driveway where the fresh tire tracks were made in the snow as the men drove out of his garage. He figured that as long as he fixed the man's car in his garage, he was safe. No harm would come to him or his family.

"We all make decisions, son," he said still looking outside. "I am not sure I have made the best decision, but it puts food on the table for you and your siblings. This man pays us very well." Slowly he let his eyes move from the car tracks and back to his son. "As you get older you will also have to make decisions. You will have to weigh out the consequences in your head and hope the decisions you've made were the right ones."

Antonio leaned on a car with his arms crossed as he listened. He never let his eyes stray from his dad.

"You understand, don't you, son?" John asked as he strolled toward him.

Antonio nodded.

"Come on, son. Let's get cleaned up for dinner." He said resting his arm on his son's shoulder leading him toward the house.

Chapter Five

We Meet Again

April was unusually cold, but anticipation was building for the baseball game between the Chicago Cubs and the Cincinnati Reds. The parking lot was full of fans walking to the stadium at Wrigley Field. The wind swiftly rolled off Lake Michigan. One neat thing about Wrigley was that every seat was a good one and close to all the action. After being pushed and shoved by the anxious crowds, Mike, Darlene, and Rosemary found their seats. With the tradition of singing the Star-Spangled Banner, the game began.

The Chicago Cubs jogged quickly to their positions. First up to bat was Cincinnati Red player, Pete Appleton. Guy Bush started Appleton off with a high inside fastball. Ball one. His next pitch was low and over the middle of the plate. Appleton got a piece of it, sending a weak ground ball to short resulting in a 6 to 3 putout.

Next up was Hughie Critz. Bush started him off with a lazy fastball over the outside of the plate. Critz smacked it up the middle for a single. Next up was Ethan Allen. He took more than the usual time getting ready in the batter's box and Bush was noticeably agitated. Finally ready, Bush let loose with a blazing inside fastball that brushed Allen's back. The crowd went wild. Allen settled back into the box and shot a scowl in Bush's direction. Bush's next pitch was a hanging curve ball that Allen crushed to right field for a single, sending Critz to third base.

A man on first and third, one out – it was cleanup hitter, Val Picinich's, turn at bat. He slapped Bush's first pitch to Hod Ford at second base, which bobbled it for an error. Critz held at third. The bases were loaded. The fans were getting nervous. Next up was Jack White. Bush reared back and fired a low outside fastball. White took that pitch for ball one. Bush's next offering was a sharp inside slider. White hit a wicked groundball right at Ford – an easy 5 to 6 to 3 double play to end the inning. Two hits, one error. No runs. The crowd went berserk as the Cubbies trotted off the field ready to get in their first swings.

Darlene and Mike sat in their seats yelling with excitement along with the crowd. Rosemary enjoyed the game but, wasn't really into baseball, so she decided to go to the concession stand for a hot dog and excused herself. Dragging her feet up the bleachers she let her nose tell her where the food was. As she got in line, she could smell the popcorn and noticed the clear oven with hot dogs turning around inside. There were also lots of candy bars on the racks. Only a couple of people were ahead of her, she missed the crowd. As she stood waiting for her turn, she heard a familiar voice call her name.

"Hi, Rosemary," he said with his musical voice.

She quickly spun around to find Antonio an arm's length away with a big smile on his face. She had not seen him since the day he met her at the coffee shop and later drove her home from school. She bit her lip and clasped her hands together, interlocking her fingers. She couldn't believe how anxious she was feeling just from the tone of his voice.

"Hi, Antonio," she replied nervously.

She felt a thrill go through her body as she said his name. His eyes locked with hers. Remembering how cold she reacted the first time they met, he hoped she would be a little friendlier.

"Are you enjoying the game?" He asked politely.

A smile formed on her lips as she shook her head. The line started moving again causing Rosemary to glance away and stroll to the counter. He took her smile as an invitation to get to know her. Taking a couple of steps, he made the distance between them smaller until he was standing behind her in the line. She didn't even notice until...

"What will it be?" Asked the man behind the counter.

She opened her mouth, but Antonio took over before anything came out.

"I'll take care of this," he said with authority, his eyes pleading for her to not say a word. "Two hotdogs please, with everything on them and two cokes."

Her eyes opened wide by this sudden act of generosity. Antonio handed the man some cash and in return was given the food. Turning towards her, he handed Rosemary a hot dog and coke before he led the way to some seats close to the back of the stadium. The song "Take Me Out to The Ball Game" played in the distance. They passed a couple who sang along happily. She could not help herself from following him. It was too loud to ask him where he was going. Her heart was pounding, something she had never felt before. She hoped he didn't notice. Antonio stopped at some seats in the back row. He stood waiting for her to sit before he made himself at home on the bleachers.

"Thank you," she said softly before she took her first bite.

She was secretly delighted to see him again, but tried not to show it. *How did he know she was at this event?* Rosemary had a hard time trusting men, given who her cousin was. However, this handsome boy did just buy her lunch.

All of a sudden, the crowd went wild. The cubs were at bat and Freddie Maguire hit a fly ball deep into center field making a home run. They listened to the crowd while eating their hotdogs. Antonio waited for the crowd to settle down before he spoke again.

"It is so nice to see you again, Rosemary," he commented, "and I would really like to know more about you."

Another home run! The crowd went wild.

Rosemary took another bite. Her mind wondered away for a moment and back to her parents. *They must be yelling and enjoying the hit, and probably not even missing her.* She also wondered what she could possible say that might be interesting to him.

"What would you like to know?" she asked.

He smiled. "Start from the beginning."

"Well, I was born in New York and my parents brought me here when I was really young," she began. "I have no brothers or sisters. My parents own a little corner store and while growing up, I used to help them out there."

She paused and gazed up to meet his eyes. Surprisingly, he seemed fascinated.

"There isn't much more to say," she concluded feeling her face turn warm.

"Where do you see your life going?" He asked keeping his eyes focused on hers.

She paused for a long moment to examine his face. *Was he really interested?*

"My mother says good Italian girls marry young, have babies, and cook. That is what life is all about," she added rather sadly with the sound of her mother echoing in her head.

"But you don't see life that way," he assumed. "I don't understand?" He added, his eyebrows knit together.

"I think that there's more to life than being someone's wife," she sighed and turned away. She took her finger and traced the napkin the hot dog was on before she took another bite. *Why was she explaining herself to him?*

"So you're unhappy?" He questioned with curiosity. "Aren't you looking for a husband someday?"

The crowd yelled loudly, but Rosemary and Antonio did not seem to hear them.

"Now you sound like my mother," she answered. She quickly swallowed before she went on. "Yes, maybe someday, but I want to finish school. I want to become a teacher and help people. I think there is much more to life than just being someone's wife."

His eyes squinted as he started to laugh. His laughter was not called for in her mind.

"I'm not sure I ever met a woman who wanted to get an education," he mused, causing her to grimace.

"Enough about me," she dryly interrupting his laugher. "Tell me about you."

His face softened and his eyes grew wide before he began to talk.

"I'm the son of a German-Irishman and have six brothers and sisters. I was born here on the north side of Chicago. I'm apprenticing right now with my father so I can become an auto mechanic." The smile lingered on his lips, but his eyes became serious. His head moved a little closer to hers. "And I do hope to get married and have lots of kids."

"So what were you doing by the college?" she asked petulantly. Rosemary noticeably slid her bottom to the side increasing the space between them.

"I had to go with my father to pick up a car," he explained reluctantly pulling away from her to sit up straight. "I dropped him off and was on my way back when I decided to stop at the coffee shop first."

His mind drifted back to the first time they met. How beautiful she looked sitting in the cafe and how striking she was at that moment. With penetrating eyes, he said, "Then I saw you."

Rosemary's heart skipped a beat as she listened to his words. *How can she be perturbed with him one minute and then her heart skip a beat the next?* Her mind was having trouble making sense out of this.

"Rosemary, what do you want out of life?" He asked.

The question caught her off guard. Interrupting her thoughts.

"I'm not sure," she replied. "I want to get out of this wretched town and go someplace where people are friendly without so much hatred and killing, that's for sure."

She paused a moment, closed her eyes, and drew in a deep breath. She hated what she read in the papers about her cousin Al and his band of hooligans. It seemed as though murder was their answer for everything. She didn't want any part of that life. Sure, she was grateful that he kept her parents safe, but isn't there another way to live without so much violence?

"I believe a woman can think for herself... and I plan to do that. I want to live someplace where I can walk the streets and not be afraid."

"I know what you mean," he concurred drawing a smile upon her lips.

Well they finally had something in common, she thought.

"I want to travel, maybe to Paris... to visit Europe and make a new life." He stopped for a moment and then with a languishing voice he added, "But I would miss my family if I lived so far away."

They sat quietly for a few moments with only the sounds of the crowd in the background before he turned playful.

"Of course, I wouldn't be so lonely if you came with me!"

Rosemary looked up shocked. His words took her by surprise. She just met the boy, so why would she even consider going anywhere with him? He simply stared at her, measuring her response with his eyes. His eyes traced the curve of her face with the Italian nose and the beautiful fullness of her red lips – the way her long black hair swept down her back with a brushing of some on her forehead, which showed off her big brown eyes.

It was the bottom of the fifth inning. All around them the crowd was going wild. Rosemary kept her expression under control allowing her to keep her thoughts private. She surprised herself by wanting to get to know him more, but she had been gone too long and knew her parents would be looking for her. Their eyes met and electricity charged the atmosphere between them. Antonio gazed unrelentingly into Rosemary's eyes. It wasn't until she started to get dizzy that she realized she was not even breathing. She sucked in a jagged breath and broke the silence between them before he closed his eyes.

"I need to go," she said staggering to her feet. "Thank you for the hot dog." She turned to step away.

"Rosemary?" He called, his voice sounding a little alarmed.

"Yes?"

"When am I going to see you again?" He asked flashing a huge, tooth-filled smile.

"How about Monday after school?" She suggested and before quickly departing. *Did she actually tell him to meet her at school?* She thought. The words just blurted out.

She scampered down the steps until she found the row of seats. Her mother was looking all around and finally settled down when Rosemary sat down.

"Where have you been?" The interrogation began.

With both hands Rosemary took her hair off her face and slid it behind both ears. She got a little fidgety in her seat as she acknowledged her mother's question.

"I met some kids from school," she lied. Unbeknownst to her mother, the sound of Antonio's voice and their thoughtful conversation was etched her into her heart and mind forever.

Chapter Six

Gangland Violence

It was Monday morning. Rosemary stretched, waking herself up. After jumping into the shower and quickly getting dressed, she caught the bus. Thankfully there was room for her to sit. As she relaxed, she listened to the chatter around her. It wasn't long before she exited the bus and made her way to the coffee shop for a quick cup of joe before school like always. She sat alone at a table and warmed her hands on the fresh brewed cup of coffee in front of her. She thought she caught a glimpse of a familiar face entering. As he walked closer her eyes got bigger.

"Hi stranger," the musical voice called out to her. "Can I walk you to school?" With a nod of her head, she surprised herself by saying yes. Antonio politely helped her with her coat before he grabbed her books off the table, and held the door open for her. It was a quiet walk up the block towards school. Neither Rosemary nor Antonio knew what to say. The sound of people gossiping from behind. They slowed down and let the group of students pass. A couple of girls said hi to Rosemary and she waved back.

She was careful not to glance at Antonio. His presence next to her was overwhelming. Her heart was beating so fast in her chest. The tune of a bird was heard and she tried to see it through the branches ahead. She bit her lip. Her hands went from swinging wildly by her sides to fold behind her back. She looked up and noticed no clouds seemed to etch the blue sky. His eyes trailed hers and looked up at the sky too. He didn't say a word, but smiled and stayed in step with her along the way. As they reached the steps of the school, she broke the silence.

"Thank you for carrying my books," her soft voice said as he handed them back to her. His fingers brushed hers sending glorious waves of electricity through her body livening her soul.

Gathering his courage he carefully asked. "Can I ask you something?"

"Sure."

"Let me take you out to lunch," he suggested in a quiet and convincing tone.

She glanced up at him and then turned away shaking her head. *Be responsible*, she told herself, *you don't even know this boy.*

"That's not a good idea," she replied trying to convince herself that she shouldn't go.

Antonio moved closer to Rosemary. He was careful not to touch her, but his proximity to her was more than a little stimulating. She could feel his stare. She searched her mind and told herself that she needed to go to her classes now; she didn't want to be late. Rosemary prided herself on being responsible, but there was something about him that made all of her good sense go out the window. She did agree to meet with him at the ballpark after all. She looked up into his eyes and silently pled for understanding.

"Please, let me take you to lunch?" He pushed staring longingly into her eyes. "It is only lunch, and everyone has to eat."

Rosemary bit her lip anxiously, still fighting with her more sensible side. She turned her face away from him and looked down at her books. *This is totally out of character,* she thought. *I go to school, eat lunch in the lunch room, followed by more classes before I grab the bus to go home. This is my routine but. . . . I do get an hour for lunch; and I could take that time to get to know him.* Slowly she turned to meet his gaze.

"Su-Su-Sure," she stuttered.

A broad smile stretched across his face. "Thank you," he said relieved. "I'll see you around noon."

"At noon then," she repeated. She watched as his smile got bigger before he turned to walk away. She didn't move to go into the building until she lost sight of him which mingled in with the crowd.

School that morning was difficult to concentrate on. As she sat in her English class, the sound of his voice drifted back into her mind. *'Please let me take you to lunch.'* His words rolled over and over again. In her math class, she hoped the time would pass quickly so noon would arrive and she could see Antonio again. She was having trouble understanding why she felt so anxious to see him again, when the bell finally rang pulling her out of her thoughts and back into reality.

She swiftly left the building and stopped at the top of the cement steps to see he was standing in front of a car, leaning and waiting patiently for her just as he'd promised. The sun was high in the sky leaving a shadow on his face. She paused only for a second when he noticed her and nodded his head. Carefully she stepped down the steps and towards the eyes that beckoned to her. He opened the passenger door and she slid in bashfully. She watched him move with grace as his slim body walked around the car. He looked so handsome in his black suit and bow tie. She heard him clear his throat as he got into the car.

Starting the engine, she saw a smile appear on his face while looking forward.

"Thanks for the honor of your company this afternoon," he stated as he slowly turned his face to meet her eyes.

Rosemary could not control, the color rushing to her cheeks as she smiled and nodded in return. With control he turned his head back to the street.

"I suppose you are wondering where I am taking you?" He continued.

"Yes," she said in a whisper.

"I'm going to bring you to a real nice place to eat called the Hawthorne Hotel," he announced keeping his eyes on the road. "Have you ever heard of this place?"

"Yes," she answered. "Isn't that place kind of pricy?"

She had heard her dad and Al talk about that place and how Al loved to eat meals there. Al also compared her mother's cooking to the food there, saying her mother's cooking was much better. A little voice inside her told her she needed to be careful. Her mother's words of wisdom saying don't go out with strangers kept ringing in her head. *Why did part of her want to get to know him and yet she felt like she made a mistake getting into his car?*

"A penny for your thoughts?" He said bringing her back.

She quickly glanced at him embarrassed, as if he knew what was in her mind before she turned her face toward the front of the car and concentrated on the road ahead.

When she didn't answer, he turned on the radio and they drove quietly with music from Louis Armstrong and Benny Goodman in the background.

They parked down the street and Antonio opened the car door for Rosemary. He brought forward his hand and she took it as she got out of the car. "You don't mind a little stroll to the restaurant, do you?"

She shook her head. "Thank you," her small voice said as he took her elbow and led her to the restaurant.

They walked off the cobble stone street onto the sidewalk. Rosemary lifted her chin as her eyes scanned the tall brick building. Walking past the glass windows, she could see some reflections of tables. He opened the door for her. Upon walking in, they passed a little post office like area. Little boxes lined the walls. Some of which had letters inside. There was a reception desk in front of the mailboxes where one could rent a room for the night. Past that was a doorway, and to the right was the beautiful restaurant.

The hotel amazed Rosemary with its beautiful chandeliers and pretty, red flowery drapes that matched the carpeting when they arrived inside. Businessmen in suits and ties seemed to occupy some of the booths with an occasional couple flirting at the tables. She stood in place taking it all in.

"A table for two?" Asked the host, who was dressed in a white shirt with a black vest and tie. Antonio nodded his head as he answered with a yes.

"Very good," said the host as he picked up a couple of menus. "Follow me."

As they were escorted to a table by a window, Antonio walked close to Rosemary and held her elbow. She didn't stop him; he made her feel safe and important. Her eyes followed the host with excitement growing inside. Everything seemed surreal to Rosemary as she took in the fancy dressed people sitting and laughing while enjoying their meal. The atmosphere felt very sophisticated. A gentle, romantic melody hung in the air. It was all like something from a dream. The pictures on the walls look like something you would see at an art gallery. The table they were escorted to had a beautiful red table cloth, with white plates that had red folded cloth napkins on top. The glasses on the table were glowing with tiny prisms as the sun hit them.

"Will this be all right?" Asked the man as he waved his hand in front of the table.

Antonio smiled and looked around the room taking in the view as well. He shook his head no before he spoke.

"How about something more private?" He inquired.

They shared a glance and with a nod of his head, the host led them around a partition away from the window to some secluded booths. They walked toward the back of the restaurant where they seemed invisible to the rest of the floor. It was a little darker, no window to look out of, but the table was still dressed just as pretty.

"Is this to your liking, Sir?" The host offered with another wave of his hand.

"Perfect," Antonio said.

Although the restaurant seemed full of customers and was rather noisy, the booth was private and quiet.

"Is this all right?" Asked Antonio glancing at Rosemary. She shook her head without a word. "Let's sit," he said as he stood waiting for her to side in before he slid in the other side of the booth.

"Your waiter will be right out," the host stated before he walked away.

"Well what do you think?" He whispered now that they were alone.

"It is beautiful," she replied, "I have never been to a place like this before. . . I have heard of this place, but. . . ." She stopped talking, when she almost caught herself telling him she was a relative to Al Capone, and that this was one of his favorite places to eat.

"Do you come here often?"

No was all he had time to answer when they were interrupted by the waiter.

"Hello, my name is Jake and I'll be your waiter today." He had a pleasant ring to his voice. "What can I get you to drink?"

Both of their faces turned to the voice that spoke.

He stood straight and tall with a towel draped over his right arm folded in front of him. Antonio turned quickly to Rosemary with a smile before answering the waiter.

"Two cokes please," he said without taking his eyes off of her.

"I'll be right back," the waiter replied, his eyes flickering from one to the other. Then a coy smile formed on his face as he left the table.

"So how are you today, Rosemary?" Antonio asked sincerely.

Her eyes traced his face, the square of his jaw, the soft curve of his full smiling lips, the straight line of his nose, the sharp angle of his cheekbones, the way his hair hung over his forehead. His eyes, dark, brown twinkled beneath the thick fringe of his black eyelashes. Staring into his eyes, she lost all train of thought.

"Fine," she swooned embarrassed by her response. This was a first for her. She didn't know why she agreed to come with him, or why the sound of his voice was musical to her. She was deep in thought and never noticed that she was staring at him.

He seemed amused by her. He waited for her to elaborate but the waiter appeared with their drinks before she had a chance.

"Are you ready to order?" He asked, the coy smile still on his face.

"Rosemary?" Antonio asked politely.

Her face turned red since she had not even looked at the menu. He noted the questionable look on her face and happily took charge.

"We'll each have baked ham surrounded by peas and carrots with the potato bread." He paused for a moment giving her his attention and asked, "Is that okay?"

Rosemary nodded her head in relief and the waiter left their table.

"Thank you for coming out to lunch with me today," he said starting up a conversation. He could tell she was a little reserved about being there, yet her smile let him know that part of her wanted to come.

"So, what made you decide to go to college?" He asked wanting to get to know her more.

"What's wrong with wanting an education?" She asked a little perturbed. Now he was sounding like her mother. "You want to know more about cars, don't you? Why can't I learn some kind of trade too?"

"Nothing at all," he mused. "I've just never met a woman with such dreams."

"Now you really sound like my mother," she stated aloud. "After all, times are changing. Women can vote now and hold down jobs. Just because I am a woman doesn't mean that I have to settle down, cook, get married, and have babies." She paused to take a breath. "Is there something wrong with that?" she questioned. By now, both of them were leaning in towards each other.

"Not at all," he confessed. "I think you wanting an education is one of the things that attracted me to you."

That statement put a smile on her face. She felt her face grow warm as a pink tinge colored her cheeks.

"Why thank you, kind Sir," she chuckled. "I think that is one of the nicest things you have ever said to me."

The waiter approached with their food interrupting their conversation. They both straightened up as he set the dishes down on the table.

"Is there anything else I can get you?" He asked.

"Not right now," Antonio replied. His eyes sparkled as he spoke with a serious tone. He nodded his head before letting her eyes go and his hand went for his coke. He picked up his glass, "To a wonderful new friendship."

Rosemary clinked her glass with his. She wasn't entirely sure of how she felt about this man sitting across from her, but she knew he made her smile and her heart skip a beat.

"So, tell me," he began as he cut a piece of ham. "Sounds like your mom is very good in the kitchen."

She swallowed a mouth full of food before she answered. "Yes, my mother is a very good cook. That woman can make anything into a meal that tastes fantastic."

He laughed out loud. "And you don't want to be like that?"

She politely took the napkin and patted her lips. "No, Sir, I am a 1920's woman and we don't have to stay in the kitchen."

"I take it that you can't cook," he chuckled again. "And if I married you, I would have to learn to cook while you were in schools teaching children how to read and write?"

"No, not at all," she replied smugly. "I, Sir, am a very good cook. My mother has this love for cooking and baking that I will never understand, yet she has passed the art of cooking on to me." Rosemary lifted her fork and shuffled her food around the plate. A frown had creased her delicate face. "I guess that is why she can't understand why I don't feel the same way."

"What do you mean?"

"She only wants the best for me and she is so proud that I have a high school education. She told me that good, Italian, catholic girls get married young and have babies. For most that is what life is all about. But. . ." Her voice trailed off.

"But you feel different," he said finishing her sentence.

"Maybe you do understand," slowly escaped from her mouth before she took another bite.

As they were eating their meal, Rosemary noticed a familiar figure out of the corner of her eye. The man looked around the room. She hid her face with her hand not wanting her cousin to get a glimpse of her, but it was too late. She watched his eyes glance toward Antonio before returning to her with an unsettled look.   His eyes had a note of disapproval in them. Now she knew she was in trouble.

Al walked in with a bodyguard and grabbed a table by the window.   Rosemary shifted uneasy her seat. She slid downward like she was trying to escape or hide. Antonio could not help noticing the difference in her body language.

"Have you changed your mind?" He asked uncomfortably. "Do you wish for me to take you back now?"

Her eyes flashed up to his face confused.

"I was only teasing you," he stated. "I didn't mean any harm."

"What?" She squeaked. Part of her then wished she were at school. *Did Al recognize her? Would he tell her parents?* The tug of what her parents would think if they found out she was with a man they didn't know was a little more than she could handle at the moment. A little voice inside of her whispered that she needed to be careful. Frustrated with herself, she took a deep breath. *Relax,* she told herself as she watched Al sit down. *If he knew it was you, he would have come over to see who you were sitting with.*

Her eyes locked on Antonio's and in a soft voice she replied, "Of course I'm glad to be here with you. I don't want to leave just yet." Part of that was true. Rosemary wanted to get to know

Antonio better. The other part was afraid of getting caught on a date by her cousin Al.

As she enjoyed the conversion and food, she soon forgot about her troubling cousin, and enjoyed her time with Antonio. They ate and they talked. They discussed her classes in school and about the cars that Antonio worked on. She caught herself laughing out loud a couple of times, bringing up the napkin to her mouth to quiet the sound. The music still played quietly in the background, but it seemed like they were all alone. The fantasy of the place took a hold of her and his presence eased her mind like all was well with the world.

"I love to hear you laugh," were the last words she heard from Antonio. Her fantasy came to a halt, as the sound of guns firing in the street echoed throughout the restaurant. Al's bodyguard, Frankie Rio, threw Al to the floor and covered him with his body. He took out his gun and held it firmly – ready and waiting to use it.

Antonio grabbed Rosemary and they also hit the floor. He pulled her under the table wrapping his body around her. The loud sound scared her causing her scream. She buried her face in his chest as he held her tight. Although it was only moments, it seemed like minutes before the shooting stopped. Soon Al and Frankie arose from the floor. Everything became quiet – an uncomfortable quiet – until the sound of roaring motors from cars drove toward the hotel. Rosemary tried to move, but Antonio would not let her get up yet. He was afraid of what might happen next.

Antonio also saw the man that walked into the restaurant and he recognized him from the papers. The words of his father rang in his ears. *'You have to make decisions son, and you hope they are the right ones.'* He thought of what his father said about George Moran and Al Capone fighting to take control of the city.

The sound of bullets rang out amid the chaos. Rich, dark plumes of smoke filled the air as each magazine emptied from the Tommy guns. The crashing of breaking glass echoed in the air along with screams of people trying to avoid being hit. Rosemary put her hands over her ears in horror as Antonio tried to shield her from passing bullets. The cars parked along the streets were riddled with holes in their doors and windows.

Frankie threw Al back down onto the floor as bullets passed through the restaurant's walls and shattered its windows. A metallic rickshaw sound flew through the building with the fast whistling and wining of bullets passing their ears. Glasses and plates fell to the floor in pieces sending shards across the dining room that looked like snow. A stray bullet shattered the vase of flowers that sat on the table beside Rosemary and Antonio. Water spilled to the floor as flowers rained down upon them. Rosemary coward deeper into Antonio's chest. It seemed as if this shooting spree would never end.

Wanting Al dead, Pete Guesenberg, one of Bugs' men, stepped out of his car with his Tommy gun in hand, walked up to the hotel and began shooting. Wearing a khaki army shirt and brown overalls, he knelt in front of the doorway and emptied a 100-round capacity drum into the restaurant before he casually walked back to his car. Lamps were hit and crashed to the floor. Bullets tore through the mail slots shredding the parchment. Letters floated to the ground in a grizzly mess. The mirror on one wall shrieked as it broke into a million pieces. The pictures on the walls that were painted so beautifully were destroyed by gaping holes. The paneled wood wall looked like Swiss cheese by the time Pete was done. More smoke blanketed the air.

The restaurant patrons were clearly frightened. All of whom hid on the floor beneath the tables like Rosemary and Antonio tried to do. Then just as quickly as the barrage began, it ended. Pieces of glass still struck the floor and muffled screams could be heard. Frankie got up first with his gun out and ready in case he needed to use it. He noticed the others on the floor covered in glass too scared to get up. He nodded to Al. Al stood up and looked around the room. His eyes touched upon everyone lying, on the floor but he didn't see Rosemary. Frankie prodded him to get a move on, so without delay they cautiously left the restaurant.

One by one people rose and helped each other to ensure no glass shards remained on them. Antonio got up on his knees allowing Rosemary to sit up. Tears streaked down her face and her body shook uncontrollably. On the floor holding each other, she cried.

"It's okay, Rosemary," he said attempting to reassure her. She didn't hear him. The

64

echoing of the guns still rang in her ears. If she hadn't left school, she would not have had to witness this event.

With her face still buried in his chest, he stroked her hair. She had never felt so frightened before. This man, whom she only had just met, made her feel safe. The feeling of being frightened and safe at the same time was hard to comprehend. Slowly, Antonio put his hands-on Rosemary's shoulders and stood up bringing Rosemary with him. The sight before them was unbelievable. Tables were turned on their sides and table clothes had been thrown to the floor. Shattered glass covered the carpet and food was strewn all over. Holes imprinted the walls that were once so beautifully decorated and a smoky residue lingered in the room. Some people were crying for help, others looked like they were in shock, while a few still helped each other get rid of glass pieces that hit their bodies. The waiters rushed around looking to see who needed medical care. As Rosemary examined the room, she imagined the bullets flying and hitting whatever got in there way. She heard the rickshaw sound in her mind that now haunted her. Up ahead where the beautiful chandelier was hanging now remained a light fixture with missing and broken glass. The fantasy was over.

Then it occurred to her, would this have anything to do with her cousin Al? She read the papers and knew of the war between him and Moran, but at a time like this, while innocent people were having lunch? Could this really be happening? She looked around and didn't see Al or his body guard. Her cousin didn't even come by to see if she was safe. Maybe he didn't see her after all. Her face turned white with her next thought. *What would Antonio think of her if he knew that Al was her second cousin?*

They slowly walked through the torn restaurant, helping people along the way, to help them stand, to sit, or wipe blood off their faces. The broken glass crumbled under their feet. It was everywhere.

Cautiously, Antonio held Rosemary's shaken form and led her out of the building. What else could she do but follow him? He was the only thing at the time that made her feel safe and secure. Staying close together, they walked quickly down the street to his car. Luckily, he had parked far enough away that no bullets had struck it.

***

Bugs thought he finally had a chance to kill Al. His anger for the man ran deep. He had previously held a meeting with his boys and carefully went over his plan. Bugs and his men kept a close eye on Al so they knew where he would be and when to strike. Al fancied himself a man of the people. He was a predictable man. Finding him would be an easy task. Bugs figured Al would be least expecting an assault and most vulnerable while eating. He arranged to have ten cars drive slowly past the Hawthorn Hotel around noon. His men would have their Tommy Guns aimed out the car windows. As the cars rolled by, they would let him and his goons have it. Bugs didn't care who got in the way. He wanted Al Capone dead!

***

"Do you want to go back to school?" Antonio asked as they sat in his car. He observed her as she tried to compose herself and added, "I'm so sorry I took you here, Rosemary."

She took a deep breath sucking in some air before she tried to speak. Her voice was stuck in her throat. The intensity of the experience over shadowed her wit. This was something she would maybe read about, not experience. It occurred to her that lunch time was well over due and she was already late for classes. Finally, she gathered enough courage to speak.

"It's not your fault," she replied with a frown.

Rosemary gazed out the car window, her mind going over and over what had just happened. Looking down the street, she could see cars in front of the restaurant filled with bullet holes. She knew that if anyone was in them, they must be hurt. When she spotted police cars and ambulances racing up the street to attend to any victims, she realized just how lucky she had been. She closed her eyes and took another deep breath. She had read in the newspaper about drive-by shootings, but never figured she'd be involved in one. It was just the kind of violence she had hoped to avoid. Now more than ever she wanted out of this place and away from all the violence.

Then it occurred to her, this man sitting next to her saved her life. He really didn't know her, yet he shielded her away from bullets and falling debris. The thought of someone with so much courage overwhelmed her. No one ever did anything like this before or treated her with so much gentleness.

"Thank you for covering me with your body so I wouldn't get hurt," she whispered. The words hurt her throat as she pushed herself to say them. The words hung in the air. She glanced up at him as she brushed a strand of hair behind her ear.

Her eyebrows creased and a puzzled look crossed her face. "You don't even know me, yet you saved my life and were willing to give yours."

Rosemary could barely fathom someone doing something so brave. He put his body over hers to protect her, even if it meant that he would have been shot and possibly killed himself. *How does one react to that?*

"You don't feel it?" He asked searching her face with the hope she felt the same about him as he did about her. For the first time his soul had peace. He couldn't help but be drawn to her. His feelings for her were so strong. He could feel love, joy and happiness right down to his bones.

The words he spoke did not make sense to her. She looked at him wide eyed. *What was it he wanted her to feel?* She was frightened beyond belief.

"I feel terrible that this had to happen," he continued as his fingers turned red from squeezing the steering wheel. "If anything had happened to you..."

Antonio started up the car. His foot hit the accelerator and the car wheels squealed out of the parking space. His foot pressed the gas pedal forcefully. His mind tried to grasp the reality of what just happened. As his pulse raced, the speedometer went higher.

Rosemary turned her attention to the road and wondered what he was talking about as the words *don't you feel it* echoed in her mind. If it wasn't enough that they were just in a shootout, now they may get into a car wreck because of his fast driving. Rosemary, still shaken, glanced toward the man behind the wheel, the same man who put his body over hers to keep her alive, and on an impulse, she let her hand touch the top of his. His skin tingled beneath her fingertips. She felt the strain in his hand when she first touched him. Her eyes never left his face. His eyebrows bore close to his nose as he kept his eyes straight ahead looking only at the road. She never said a word, but at the moment she considered to pick up her hand she noticed his face to relax a little. His hand loosened on the wheel. She decided to keep her hand on his if it was helping in any way to soothe, him. His driving began to slow down and that was when she noticed she was holding her breath. They drove around for a little while, no talking, and no radio, just the sound of the car engine and whatever was going on in their heads.

"Do you want to go back to school?" the once musical voice, now strained asked.

"No," she relied, quietly looking forward. Her hand still rested gently on his.

"Do you want me to take you home?"

She hesitated. She was too shaken up to see her parents right now. "No."

"Are you all right?"

"Yes," she said. "Just a little out of sorts."

"It must have been something between those two men, Capone and Moran," Antonio commented making conversation. "I've read about those two in the papers, but never thought something like this was actually real. I can't imagine how someone could go and shoot innocent people trying to get revenge. Do you think these people actually have families that care about them when they go around shooting each other?"

She leaned backwards and tried to slouch while removing her hand from his. *Would his feelings change if he knew that I was related to Al Capone?*

"Maybe their families don't know how bad they are?" she squeaked.

"You're probably right. They wouldn't show that side of themselves at the dinner table."

Antonio found himself heading to the garage where he apprenticed with his dad. Collecting herself, Rosemary felt utterly safe and totally unconcerned about where they were going. When they arrived at the garage, his father walked out to greet them.

"Hey, son, you're late!" yelled John as he approached the car. Looking into the front of the car he noticed a woman sitting next to his son. "Well, well. Whom do we have here?" He added with a broad smile.

Antonio got out of the car and walked around to open Rosemary's door. His eyes were hard and his body stiff. She looked up at him with a comforting smile, which seemed to ease his disposition.

"Well now, I understand why you got all dressed up, son," he laughed.

"Dad, this is Rosemary," Antonio said taking her hand gently and helping her out of the car.

"Rosemary, this is my father, John."

John stretched out his hand to her.

"Nice to meet you," she replied searching his face and seeing the resemblance here. His kind smile and deep brown eyes were almost like looking at Antonio only a few years older with a few strains of grey at the temples. His hand shake was sincere just like his smile.

"I suppose he wants to show off what he's been doing to these fine vehicles," John chuckled as he led them inside. His voice had the same tone as Antonio, but it was missing something which didn't make it musical like Antonio's. His tall lean body walked into the garage not waiting for them but assuming they were following him.

"You okay?" he asked, peering up at her. Slowly she nodded her head yes.

Antonio shrugged his shoulders while looking at Rosemary and waved his hand across his body for her to enter first.

"Shall we?" He said letting his hand grasp hers.

She did not resist as their fingers
intertwined.

Chapter Seven

A Dangerous City

Chicago seemed to be the place for mob
warfare and perfect location for a criminal
empire. There was a vast enterprise that Al

Capone, leader of the South Side outfit and George 'Bugs' Moran, leader of the North Side gang bought into, full of violent people, bootlegging, gambling houses, saloons, and police corruption. Thus the city became famous for its sexual promiscuity and its wealth. Innocent bystanders were not safe. Accidental shootings were a daily occurrence and many lives were lost all in the name of rivalry.

Always dressed in the finest clothes, Al was known to attend operas, sporting events, and even charitable functions with the public. He was friendly, generous, and successful. And to the rowdy crowds that drank bootleg alcohol, he seemed almost respectable.

Moran was known more for his temper and earned the nickname Bugs, which is street slang for 'completely crazy.' He took control of the breweries and distilleries on the north side of the city. His gang also burglarized local stores and warehouses, and ran illegal gambling operations. They also secretly hijacked beer shipments from the south side and then sold the beer back to them.

Both of the gangs were greedy and territorial. They wanted to gain control over the city's bootlegging and gambling profits, which led to open warfare.

It was Bugs who called a meeting with his boys to formulate a plan to put Al out of business for good. They all sat down in a hotel suite while Bugs got a drink from the room's bar. Frank and Pete, the Gusenberg brothers, were there, as well as Albert Weinshank, James Clark, Adam Heyer, and Dr. Reinhart Schwimmer.

They were dressed in dark suit jackets, with matching vests and pants, white or black band fedora hat, with a contrasting tie. The men sat at their leisure smoking cigars and sipping bourbon, waiting to hear what George had to say.

"I remember it like it was yesterday," he began as he walked away from the bar with a fresh drink in his hands. He was still in mourning over Dean and vowed to seek revenge for the death of his friend.

He placed a finger in his drink and moved it in circles while watching the ice spin.

"I dropped him off that morning at the Schofield Flower Shop. I told him to be careful of the Gennas," he sighed. "He laughed," Bugs chuckled darkly. "He never saw it coming."

***

Dean strolled into his flower shop; he scooped a rose from a vase on the counter, and put the bud on his lapel. This day seemed like any other day. Then he closed his eyes and drew a deep breath to smell the aroma of the roses and carnations. The sun poured in past a row of flowers in front of the main window creating shadows across the floor. The little bell on the top of the door rang as it opened and three customers entered the small shop. Dean turned around and smiled as he greeted the gentlemen like he always had done. They wore pinned stripped suits with ties and matching hats. Big grins swept across their faces as they walked up next to him. The man in the middle extended his hand.

"Ah, good morning' boys," Dean said extending his hand in return. "What can I do for you?"

As soon as their hands touched, the other two men took out their guns and started to shoot. A loud metallic sound echoed through the little shop as a bullet hit Dean's chest and he fell to the floor. Then just to make sure he was dead, one of the men stood directly over him and shot a bullet into his head.

***

"We will make him pay," Bugs said angrily walking in circles around the room. "Capone is going to die." Moran took a big swig from his glass.

"How are we going to do that?" Frank asked spreading his arms wide. "He has the Gennas to protect him." A couple of whispers that seemed to agree with Frank floated across the room when he spoke. "You're right." were some of the words mumbled in the room.

Bugs disliked being questioned. Walking around the room his eyes peered at each of the boys making them feel very uncomfortable, before stopped in front of Frank. With all his strength, he yanked Frank up out of his chair by the collar of his shirt. Bugs' eyes bored into him as if they were daggers. Frank stared wide-eyed with fear as his body involuntarily was brought into a standing position. A few gasps were heard faintly around them.

"Don't ever question what I tell you to do again!" Bugs shrieked. He looked around the room. "That goes for all of you."

He shoved Frank back down into his chair and got the attention of the whole group.

"He's not more powerful than us," He growled. He paused for a moment to gather his thoughts. The other men watched in fear as his body began to twitch and his eyes squinted, his eyebrows lowering into his nose.

"Two can play this game. . . " Was all Bugs' whispered before his head shot up and his eyes grew big. An idea came to him. He had the look of a madman and the fear began to increase within his gang. "We will start by getting rid of Pasqualino Lolordo," He announced shaking a fist in the air like a lunatic. "Pasqualino takes care of Al. What if the head of the Sicilians is gone?" he added with an evil smile. "Then it would be easier to get Al." A wicked smile stretched from ear to ear. Bugs' was clearly pleased with his own genius.

***

Meanwhile the sound of jazz became one of the most popular sounds in Chicago. The night clubs were booming with people dancing to the perfect democracy of the saxophone, trumpet, trombone, piano, bass, drums, and guitar. The city soon had many underground jazz clubs where people could drink and dance without the fear of being caught. If there ever was a place to get away and forget life for a while it would be in one of these clubs. It wasn't fondly referred to as the roaring twenties for nothing. It quickly became the era of the flapper. The women wore dresses just below the knees so that when they danced the Charleston part of their knee would show. Men wore slim suits with tight jackets that had sloping shoulders and bow ties were becoming fashionable. It seemed like the sound of Louis Armstrong or Benny Goodman took your mind away for a while to someplace fun forgetting all the tragedy around you.

***

As for Rosemary, her days began at the coffee shop where she met Antonio before school. She kept herself busy studying and working toward her college degree. Her evenings were consumed with helping her mother to cook and taking care of chores around the house.

Sometimes Al would come over for dinner to enjoy the friendship of her father and of course, her mother's cooking.

It was the first time Rosemary had seen him since the shooting. When he went to kiss her hello, she stopped cold in her tracks and in a very low voice told him not to touch her again. He looked around the room to make sure no one was in sight when he grabbed her arm.

"Look here, young lady," he scolded, his beady eyes taking a hold of hers. "I bet your parents don't even know you skipped school that day, do they?"

"No, they don't," she answered, her voice in a low growl. "So, was I in the middle of one of your fights with Bugs? Is that what you two do, shoot each other and any innocent person that happens to be in the way?"

She tried to jerk her body away from him, but he was too strong. She could feel his grip getting tighter. "What, are you going to hurt me now too?" She snapped. She thought she saw a spasm of pain flicker across his face as her words made their way to his ears. "You didn't even stay to see if I was all right," she accused.

"It's complicated," he answered. "You know I love you and your family. I would never want anyone or anything to hurt you." His grip loosened up on her arm.

"What is the name of the boy you were with?" He continued. "How do I know whether or not it was your boyfriend who planned for me to get shot?"

"What?" Her surprised voice said.

"You know it was Moran who wanted you dead." She said. He remained quiet; his eyes intent upon her face. "You also can't say anything to my parents, not unless you want me to let them know you left me for dead." She jerked her body away one more time and freed herself. "The boy I was with is a hero," she went on. "He covered me with his body to protect me. That's more than I can say about you." The more anxious she became the more she pronounced her words slow and individual. Her eyes piercing up at him.

"I want to know who the boy is you were with!" He ordered. "I am now afraid for your life. What if he is a part of Moran's group and he is using him to get to me?"

She was hesitant by his words and let them sink into her brain. "What do you mean?" She now asked in a soft voice. Her shoulders starting to relax.

"You remember how your grandparents died, don't you? . . . They were my family too, and I often stayed with them. There death is on my conscience. Those bullets were meant for me. I brought your family here to be safe and I don't want anything to get in the way of your safety Rosemary."

Rosemary looked up into Al's eyes and saw how the anger left them leaving them vulnerable. She knew he was right. He didn't want any harm to come to her and her family, yet at the same time she could not understand how he chose to live this way.

"Don't worry about the boy I was with," she whispered as her eyes softened. "He doesn't own a gun or have a mean bone in his body. And we think alike, we don't like fighting."

Darlene walked in with a plate of spaghetti noticing the two of them close enough to be talking in whispers.

"Ready to eat?" She asked as she placed the plate on the table. Al and Rosemary, their eyes still on each other, both shook their heads and said "yea" in a quiet tone before letting their eyes go. Each of them going to the table to eat like a family with no mention of what had happened.

Rosemary harbored a secret dislike for Al, especially after the shooting at the restaurant, but for her parent's sake, she was always on her best behavior. After all, Al did help her parents out with the corner store and his boys kept them safe. In a sense you could say, she had a love/hate feeling for the man. She did not respect what he did for a living. It was easy to figure out simply by reading the local newspaper. But she also respected her parents, even if that meant being nice to Al.

On most days, Rosemary got a ride home from school with Antonio. She came up with various excuses so they could spend more time together. Antonio was not Italian and she worried about whether she should tell her parents about him.

"When are you going to meet a nice Italian boy and get married," her mother would say.

She knew that sooner or later, she would have to tell them, but just not yet. She wanted to get to know him without their added pressure.

Antonio kept busy working in his father's garage and learning more about auto mechanics. He often worked all day long, so he could take off early to spend a few hours with Rosemary. Bugs' boys paid visits whenever they needed something special done to their cars, which meant exceptionally good pay. Yet Antonio wondered if they were the ones who came to the restaurant with all that gun power. He thought that he noticed Capone walking in the restaurant with one of his men before the shooting. He also remembered how uncomfortable Rosemary became after that thug walked in. That day will always haunt him.

One morning as Rosemary hurried to get dressed for school, her mother knocked on her bedroom door.

"Mama?" She asked while slipping on her dress.

Her mother opened the door slowly before taking a step inside.

"Aren't you going to be late for work?" Rosemary asked. She noticed the frown on her mother's face.

Her mother did not respond. Rather she stood quietly watching her daughter, making Rosemary feel uncomfortable. As Rosemary zipped up the back of her dress, she took a big breath. She didn't look at her mother but could see her out of her peripheral.

"Rosemary, you don't always come home right after school," she finally said causing Rosemary to turn away embarrassed.

She never kept anything from her mother before and instantly felt guilty. She knew in the back of her mind that this conversation would eventually arise.

"Are you seeing someone?"

Rosemary scuttled around the room trying to finish getting dressed buying herself time to gather her wit. She put on her watch. Next, she picked up the long fake white pearl necklace and placed it around her neck. Finally, she picked up a brush to do her hair before she answered. She did not want to lie, but telling her the truth did not seem like a good option either. Her mother waited patiently resting her eyes on her daughter's face. Finally, Rosemary turned to face her.

"Mama, I wanted to tell you," she said studying her mother's face.

The lines under her mother's eyes showed her age a little more that day she thought and felt another pang of guilt.

Am I the reason she looks like that? She wondered.

Her mother moved toward her, took the brush from her hand, and made smooth strokes through Rosemary's long black wavy hair.

"I remember when you were small and I brushed your hair every day for you," she said with a somber look.

"I remember, Mama," Rosemary quickly replied. "We always counted to one hundred."

She brushed a few more strokes to her hair bringing back past memories of the child she once had.

"You know that you're still my baby," she said quietly, wrapping her arms around Rosemary's shoulders. Darlene let her cheek fall on her daughter's cheek. Rosemary closed her eyes and crossed her arms bringing her hands up to touch her mothers. She knew her mother always knew when she was hiding something.

"He's a good boy, Ma," Rosemary whispered softly. "You would like him."

Her mother kissed her on the top of her head. "Will I get to meet him soon?" She asked as her arms slipped off Rosemary's shoulders.

Rosemary simply shook her head 'yes' causing her mother to smile.

As usual Antonio waited for Rosemary at the coffee shop. He had a hot cup of steaming brew waiting for her on the table. His eyes widened as she sauntered through the front

door.   She   wore   a   navy-blue   dress   which
gathered at the hips and a fell with a print of
flowers rested from her hips to just below her
knees.

He instantly jumped up. "Good morning,"
he said with a smile and pulled out a chair for
her.

"Good morning!" Her eyes twinkled at the
sight of him.

Antonio had on his work clothes, a white
buttoned-down   shirt   with   pockets   on   each
breast and dark pants. He still looked good to
her, even in those clothes. Rosemary sat down
and took the hot cup in her hands to warm them.

"Thank you."

"My pleasure," he smiled teasingly as he
took his seat.

"So, what did you do last night?"

"Helped my mother with dinner and went
straight to my homework," she said after she
took a sip. She could feel him starring at her.
"And my mother wants to meet you," she slipped
in the conversation.

His face instantly lit up. *Maybe he was
finally going to meet her parents*, he mused.
This could be a good sign.

"And what did you do last night?" The
angelic voice asked before he had a chance to
say anything about her last remark.

"I did some tinkering on cars and helped
my parents with my siblings."

"It must be fun to have so many brothers
and sisters." She sighed resting her chin on her
hand, and her elbow on the table.

"Yea, it is," he laughed out loud. "We have lots of tickle fights and chase each other around the house. Of course, someone always ends up getting hurt and then the fights begin. You can't have fun without someone getting mad or hurt."

"I wonder what that would be like."

"Who knows," his sly voice said, "maybe someday you will find out."

Her nose crinkled up as she shook her head. "I don't think so. I think my mother is way beyond having any more kids."

"I didn't mean it that way," he said with a hint of laughter in his voice.

Her face shot up with a confused look. He shrugged his shoulders with a sly smile. She withdrew her eyes from him and towards her coffee. Picking up the cup she took another swig.

"Do you have any plans after school today?"

Meeting his gaze, she forgot about the conversation she just had with her mother. "No," she replied and his smile brightened even more.

"Good," he said tapping his fingers on the table. "I have someplace special I want to take you."

"Where?" She asked while staring into his brown eyes.

"It's a surprise," he said excitedly. "Come on, let me walk you to school so you won't be late and I will meet you when you are finished with your classes."

She took one last sip before standing up to leave.

Antonio took her books for her. The sun was bright and high in the sky feeling warm on their faces. They mixed with the other students walking the same way. Some girls saying hi to them before they ran ahead to meet others.

"Aren't you going to tell me where you are taking me?" She asked turning her body to face him batting her eyelashes.

He walked closer to her, studying her face. His heart did a summersault as he peered into her eyes. "No," he whispered, into her ear. "It's more fun this way."

Her shoulders dragged as she looked away and listened to his laughter.

The day seemed to go by slowly as Rosemary focused her mind on her studies. She could not help thinking of Antonio and the surprise he had waiting for her. When the school day ended, she walked outside. Leaning on his car, with light gray pants and a matching vest, white shirt, black tie, and hat, Antonio stood with his ankles crossed waiting patiently. She admired him from afar before stepping towards him. As she drew closer, he rushed up to her and took her books from her arms. Then he smiled slightly and kissed her on the cheek. The sweet gesture sent shivers up her spine. Color instantly flooded her cheeks. She smiled and followed him to his car.

"Well, where are you taking me?" Rosemary asked settling into the passenger seat.

Antonio put on the car radio and kept turning the knob until he heard the tune he wanted to find.

"Have you ever heard this music before?" He asked as the wonderful sound of jazz streamed forth.

"Oh sure," she said, "everyone knows him. That's Louis Armstrong."

Antonio leaned his head against the car seat and smiled.

"That's my girl," he said as he drove snapping his fingers to the beat of the music.

They arrived at the Sunset Café, one of the most popular jazz clubs in Chicago. Walking inside, they checked their coats and a host led them to a table. The walls were white with little lamps extending from them shining a delicate light on the tables below. The joint was in full swing.

People laughing and talking with cigarette smoke hanging in the air. Girls wearing tight little outfits walked around selling cigarettes and drinks. As they sat down, one of the girls arrived at their table with a menu.

"What can I get you?" She asked in almost a yell to be heard over the music.

"A beer and a coke please," said Antonio.

As the waitress rushed away to get their drinks, Rosemary's eyes opened wide scanning from one side of the room to the other. There were several tables circling a dance floor. At each of them, men and women were drinking, smoking, talking, and laughing. A fog of smoke passed over the dance floor where a few couples were doing the Charleston. Rosemary also noticed ten dark-skinned men on the stage. Six of them played shiny brass instruments swaying them up and down as the beautiful music came out of them. One gentleman played a guitar, while another tickled the ivory keys, and a silver tongue dame sang her heart out. The placed was hopping.

"Well," Antonio said to get Rosemary's attention, "what do you think?"

She glanced back at him, her eyes shining with excitement. She felt like she was again back in heaven. Still part of her was not at ease. She told her mother she would introduce this boy to her. She would have to lie about where she was at when she got home. But the atmosphere put that thought in the very back of her mind.

"This is wonderful."

They stared deeply into each other's eyes, lost in each other's gaze, drowned in the sound of the music, and overcome by the frenzy of the crowd.

"Come on," Antonio said rising from his chair.

He put his hand out to her never letting his eyes leave her angelic face. Gladly, she took his hand and he led her onto the dance floor. He put his right arm around her waist and took her right hand in his left. The beat of the music took over and their feet stepped to the lively beat. Rosemary loved dancing to the sound of the brass and piano.

"You're not a bad dancer," she snickered amazed at how well he knew the steps.

"You're not bad either," he said smiling.

Then he tried to show off by making her do a couple of twirls. The dance floor thumped loudly to the beat and the movement of many feet. It seemed like a different time and place as they danced and laughed without a care in the world. The music spun around them lifting away gravity. He watched her hair spin out and bounce more with each move and beat.

The tempo of the next song was slow. Rosemary looked up at him expectant to follow. Antonio held her gaze as he drew her close. Ever so slowly, they began to move to the music, turning in measured circles. The slow music twirled like a thread around them.

Rosemary was barely conscious of the other couples joining the dance floor around them. She took a deep breath as he gently put both arms around her waist. As the music played in the background, Rosemary put her arms around his shoulders and let her head lean against his chest as she let him sway her body around and around. Rosemary could feel his heart beating and smell his cologne. Antonio closed his eyes as she put her head on his shoulder. She felt so safe and secure as they swayed back and forth to the music. At that instant nothing else mattered. Not her parents, or the unjust shootings, only this.

"Are you having fun?" He asked, his lips almost touching her ear.

Chills ran through her body and her heart pounded. She felt his body press against hers as they moved in slow, small circles on the dance floor. As she raised her head to look into his eyes, their cheeks accidentally touched and it felt as if an electric current passed between them. Her eyes said it all without her uttering a word. His eyes penetrated into hers before he lowered his face and let his lips touch hers. He felt her body tremble so he held her even tighter.

Rosemary was dizzy with the intense emotions going through her that she never felt before. She molded into his kiss and forgot about the curious eyes around them. Her breath became a wild gasp as she parted her lips for him. Her fingers knotted into his hair, clutching it firmly. Overcome with desire, he clutched her dress by her waist pulling her into him. He slowly and gently let her lips go, but refused to let her move. His eyes were inches from her face and full of excitement. He grinned with satisfaction as he casually loosened his grip. They continued to dance and spin.

For a moment they were lost in a world that seemed to be created just for them. He continued to hold her close moving slowly on the dance floor until the music stopped. Then he led her back to their table.

"Rosemary," he said with a playful smirk, "you have intoxicated me by your very presence."

He gazed into her eyes and felt encouraged by them. She was lost in his stare and could not respond. He watched as she slid her finger across her cheek and tucked hair behind her ear. Her fingers followed her hair down to her shoulders. Still not a sound came out of her mouth. She tried to speak but nothing came out. Her heart was bursting in her chest and she wondered if he could hear the beats.

"Are you not affected at all by this?" He asked quizzically as he tried to read her face.

At that point, conflicting thoughts entered her mind. She remembered the conversation she had with her mother that morning, but was also dazed by the kiss she shared with Antonio just seconds before on the dance floor. She then recalled him sheltering her from flying bullets at the restaurant. *Who is this man and what kind of power does he hold over me? How can I resist him?* She wondered. *Am I in love with this man?*

As they both unconsciously leaned toward the middle of the table, Antonio brushed her cheek from her ear to her chin with his finger. Rosemary trembled. He heard the soft intake of her breath and waited anxiously to hear what she might say.

"Yes," she finally murmured. "I am affected by you."

His questionable look slowly turned into a smile as he lifted up one of her hands toward his lips and kissed her knuckles.

"Thank you for the honor of your company again tonight, Rosemary," he said softly. She withdrew her hand and lowered her head, hoping he didn't see her blush.

Bringing her head back up she said, "Where else would I rather be?" He laughed out loud with a smile that showed all his teeth.

Picking up his glass he said "Let's have a toast." She followed his lead putting her glass in the air. "To a wonderful relationship that I hope never ends." The words drifted to her ears and a broad smile appeared on her face as their glasses touched.

The silence left as the band returned to the stage and filled the room once again with music. Without thinking, Antonio stood up and reached for Rosemary's hand.

"Come on, baby, they are playing our song." She loved the pressure of his warm hand on her back and the feeling of her feet gliding along the floor. Her movement flowed with a dazzling grace that took his breath away. They danced for some time fully enjoying each other's company. As always good things have to come to an end.

"I had a great time," Rosemary said with a wide grin as Antonio shuffled into the driver's seat.

"So did I," he replied throwing his head back in laughter.

As she continued to look at him, he picked up her hand and pressed it lightly to his face.

"I've never seen you like this before," she said observing his behavior. He seemed so giddy. It was out of character.

"Is this not how it's supposed to be?" He smiled. *Could she not see he was carrying a torch for her?* "I feel incredible. This is love, is it not?"

Rosemary's heart did summersault and her eyes widened. She looked at his sparkling brown eyes and felt the curve of his lips under her fingertips. Goosebumps crawled down her arm as his lips touched her hand. *Is this what love feels like?* Her heart was pumping so fast she could count the beats without feeling for a pulse. When she was in school her thoughts were always on him, and not on the subject at hand. Not to mention the yearning to see him every morning, even if is just for a few moments. She had never been in love before, but if this is love, don't let it stop.

"I agree," she answered bashfully.

"Do you remember the first time we met?" He asked putting an arm around her, pulling her close. She nestled close to his body and could feel his breath as he talked. "I saw you sitting in the coffee shop." He paused for a moment, let out a snicker and continued, "There were a couple of tables free, but you were so beautiful that I had to make up an excuse to meet you."

Rosemary listened intently as he let out a deep sigh. She took his hand and let their fingers intertwine. She also remembered how cold she was to him at first. Not sure if he was a person that could be trusted.

"And then I accidentally bumped into you at the baseball game. Was that fate? I had to know."

She remembered how excited she became when he called her name. As he continued to talk, a flood of emotion filled her body. She took his hand and deliberately kissed it.

"Do you remember what you told me you wanted to do?" He asked.

"Sure," she whispered, "I told you I was going to school to become a teacher."

"You also told me something else," he grimaced.

She shook her head as she searched her mind, but had no idea what he was referring to.

"You said you wanted to get out of this awful town," he reminded her. His clear brown eyes held her in an unwavering scrutiny.

Then the memory of their talk at the ballpark came flooding back. It was the first time she actually got to know him and the first time she felt something for him. She was also impressed that he remembered their conversation. Until now, she never thought about that day at the ball park, yet it meant something to him.

"So," his words flowed swiftly now, "I was thinking we could do that. We could plan on taking a trip and move away from here. You didn't seem at the time like you would miss your parents, and even though I would miss my siblings, I want to start a life with you." He paused before he spoke again, letting go of her hand and taking his arm back to start the car. "I know this is kind of fast, but you were serious, weren't you?"

Antonio purposely looked straight ahead as he put the car into gear and his foot hit the gas pedal. He was fearful of the expression on her face. He felt like he needed to let her know what was on his mind. Rosemary was surprised that he remembered everything they talked about. She looked up at him, and saw the clenching of his jaw and his puzzled expression. She had never felt like this before or kissed a man, yet one that made her knees weak. "I know this is kind of fast," he said breaking the silence, "but I think we have clicked." His hand firmly squeezed the steering wheel. "I love you, Rosemary."

"Perhaps," she said softly. The thought of leaving Chicago was exhilarating. He did have a power over her that she could not explain. She wanted so much to be with him. Her heart pounded faster as she thought of what she should say. She was considering the possibilities of where to go and where to live or if she should stay.

"Just perhaps?" He asked as his knuckles turned white. "I don't understand. I thought you felt the same about me as I feel about you?"

"I do," she confessed. "This is kind of fast and ... kind of complicated." Her voice dropped.

"Why?" He shrugged. He continued to drive, as his hands relaxed on the wheel.

"My mother wants me to find a nice Italian boy. One that will whisk me away at this young age and take me from school and make a mother out of me. I, on the other hand, have no intentions of being a mother. . . quite yet."

"I would never ask you to quit school. In fact, that is one of the things I love about you. Your mind."

"It is also a tradition in our family that any suitor would have to ask my father for my hand in marriage. Unfortunately, I don't see him giving you his blessings."

"Rosemary," the he continued, "I will do whatever it takes."

Antonio in himself was a beautiful memory — the way he so boldly introduced himself to her at the coffee shop, how fate brought them together at the ballpark, their first deep conversation about leaving this gang-owned town, the thoughtful way he waited by his car for her and brought her to the most beautiful restaurant she had ever seen, the way he ordered on her behalf and put her at ease, and how he shielded her from the raging bullets. He would risk everything for her.

His voice was so persuasive, so hard to resist. "Yes," she finally replied.

His face immediately softened.

He turned to meet her gaze.

"Where did you have in mind," she teased pushing his face forward toward the road.

"Europe," he said enthusiastically. "Maybe Paris?"

Rosemary slid closer to Antonio and rested her head on his shoulder. Closing her eyes, she dreamed of the Eiffel Tower and how wonderful it would be to see it in person. The sun was setting and the street lights were on.

"Are you going to show me your house tonight so I can drop you off in front?" He asked. She nodded her head.

Rosemary gave Antonio the address. She reached out and pulled her fingers gently through the back of his hair as he drove her home. He felt shivers as her hand touched the back of his neck. They pulled up to her house and parked before he turned toward her.

"Thanks for a wonderful evening," he said with a loving smile.

He stroked her long hair and a shock ran through Rosemary's body. Without haste, he lifted her face and flashed his eyes up to hers for permission before he let his lips softly touch hers for a good night kiss. Gradually, his hands slid down the sides of her neck and rested on her shoulders causing her to shiver. As they continued to kiss, she caressed his cheek. When they finally parted, she traced his lips and he tried to catch his breath. Then she moved in for one more kiss before exiting the car. Antonio did not want her to go and grabbed her hand startling her.

"Tomorrow, my sweet," she said and gently drew back from him.

Rosemary ran into the house and headed up the stairs towards her room, but before she reached her room, her mother called out, "Rosemary!" She yelled from the kitchen. "Were you with him again tonight?"

She stopped in her tracks and replied, "Yes, Mama."

"When are we going to meet this young man of yours," she begged.

Rosemary recalled the conversation they had. *How was she going to explain to her mother how she felt about Antonio and that he was not Italian?* Her mother approached the bottom of the stairs and stood wiping her hands on a towel. Then she peered up at Rosemary with that look of parental authority.

"Bring him over for dinner tomorrow night," she insisted.

"Yes, Ma," Rosemary moaned. "Good night."

Chapter Eight

Meeting The Parents

The sun's rays shone through the window with beams of light settling on Rosemary's face. She felt rested from such wonderful dreams of her last few days. With a big yawn and a wide stretch of her arms, her legs rested to the side of the bed hitting the floor, before getting up. Putting on some knickers and a sailor tie blouse, she made her bed before running downstairs. On the kitchen table sat a bag of flower, sugar, and a carton of eggs. Flour was spread across the table and her mother was busy kneading dough for a piecrust. On the counter sat a bowl of wet, clean apples and a peeler.

"Ah... good morning, child," she said looking up while her hands worked on the dough and her body swayed back and forth in a rhythm. Her eyes twinkled with a touch of flour on her cheek. "I can use some help for dinner tonight," she added stopping only for a second as she pointed to the apples. "You know what to do."

Rosemary strolled towards her mom and kissed her on the cheek before stepping to the counter and picking up the peeler.

"You know, child, the best way to a man's heart is through his stomach," Darlene laughed.

"That's how I got your father to marry me."
Smiling broadly showing her teeth she added, "I
volunteered at the church for an event and was
cooking in the kitchen when your dad walked in
with a bag of apples and set them on the counter.
Being shy, I didn't acknowledge him, but he
decided to get my attention and asked me my
name." Mom blushed.

Darlene's her hands never stopped
kneading the dough as she talked. Rosemary
listened while she peeled the apples and threw
them in a bowl of water.

"So shyly, I glanced up at him," she
sighed. "He was so handsome. He didn't have a
belly like he does now," she giggled, "but then
my waist was smaller too! I told him my name and
being polite, he introduced himself. I was so
flattered." She paused for a moment to collect
her thoughts.

"Later on, when I was in the kitchen
washing the dishes, he walked in and asked me
who made the wonderful apple pie. Of course, I
told him that I did." She raised her head in the
air and closed her eyes for a moment,
remembering that day. "I can see it like it was
yesterday," she rambled on. "He took a dish
towel and started wiping the clean dishes for
me. We didn't talk much, but I enjoyed his
company. When we finished, he asked me if I
needed a way home. I told him my parents would
take me home, but then to my surprise, he asked
me if he could take me out."

Her face expressed pure happiness. "And
the rest is history," her mother sighed, the
smile never leaving her face.

"Mama," said Rosemary, "what a wonderful story."

Gathering up the apples, she got out the bread board and began to slice them.

"What about you, child," she asked as she worked on the dough. "Tell me about this mysterious man you're seeing."

Rosemary did not know how or where to start. He was good looking and kind, but not Italian. She enjoyed his company without the interrogation of her parents, but she knew they'd have to meet him eventually. She took out another apple to slice not letting her eyes leave her work.

What if they don't approve of him? She could feel her mother's eyes on her face. She could not put this off any longer.

"Ma," she finally began, "he is so nice to me. He opens the car doors, and speaks so politely with kindness."

"That's what I wanted to hear," Darlene replied shaking her head. "That he's good to you." Then she pressed on, "But wouldn't a gentleman want the woman's parents to meet him?"

"Oh, Ma, he makes me feel so special," Rosemary said closing her eyes to picture his face and releasing a soft sigh.

She did not have a story like her mother's. She had not met him in the kitchen of a church where all the other Italian Catholics congregated. He was not the same nationality or even from the same neighborhood. Darlene focused on her daughter as she talked. Then

Rosemary's face sagged into a little frown and her eyebrows knit downward.

"What is it, child?" Her mother asked.

Rosemary wrestled in her head about how to tell her. They would find out at dinner that night anyway and she did not want it to come as such a surprise.

She hesitated a moment. "Ma," she mumbled, "I don't want to disappoint you and dad."

Rosemary's eyes remained focused on her work. She was careful not to cut herself. Her mother stopped what she was doing and gave Rosemary, her full attention. Rosemary became quiet for a moment while she assembled her thoughts. The back of her neck twitched as she stressed over what words to use.

"Ma, he's so gentle and kind. You will love him," she stalled as she pushed the sliced apples in to the bowl full of water and vinegar.

Darlene started to tremble wondering what could be so bad?

"Rosemary?" Her apprehensive voice asked. "What is it that you are not telling me?" It occurred to her that maybe this boy was with the wrong crowd. *Maybe having Al hang around was a bad influence on Rosemary.* "Tell me," she went on, "where did you meet this young man?"

"By school, ma, but I don't have a story like you and dad. I am not even sure if you and dad will accept him..."

"Well, everyone has their own story, Rosemary."

"Yeah but yours is sweet and innocent. You were at church and you guys are the same religion." Then she squinted her eyes. "What if he wasn't an Italian Catholic? Would your parents still have accepted him?"

"What else would he have been? He belonged to the same parish and came from the same neighborhood. Most of my friends were Italian."

"Mom, answer the question. Would your parents let you go out with dad if he wasn't an Italian Catholic?"

Darlene didn't say a word; she shook her head no.

Rosemary shut her eyes tightly, took a deep breath and exclaimed, "Ma, he's a German-Irishman."

There, I said it, she thought as her nerves let go rippling through her body. Then her mind went crazy wondering what her mother thought. Silence filled the room for a moment, which felt like a lifetime to Rosemary. Her mother sighed out loud with relief, walked over to her daughter and wrapped her arms around her.

"Is that it? Is that all you wanted to tell me? Phew, you had me scared out of my mind. I want you to be happy, child," she said holding on to her hug.

"Really?" Tears filled Rosemary's eyes and the tenseness in her neck relaxed. "Thank you, Ma."

"Come on, Rosemary," her mother said as she turned to wipe a tear from her cheek. "We have a pie to bake."

Darlene put the dough in the pie tin. Next, she cut some more dough into long slices to place on top. Rosemary mixed some sugar, lemon juice, flour, and cinnamon. She added the mixture with the apples before she scooped them into the crust. Together they slowly placed the long slices of dough over the pie into a crisscross weaved pattern.

"Wait till I tell him you made this pie!" Exclaimed Darlene excitedly. "You may be getting married soon!"

"I know, ma," Rosemary said as she sulked at the table, resting her head in her hands. "All good catholic Italian girls get married young and have babies. But, ma, I am not sure I am ready for marriage yet."

Darlene put the pie into the oven and sat down next to her.

"I am not sure how dad is going to take the idea that he is not Italian." Her eyes locked with her mom's.

"Let's not worry about that until tonight when he meets him," Darlene said in a convincing tone.

"We don't have a story like you and dad," said Rosemary. "He is not going to fall in love with me because of my apple pie."

Mom sighed out loud, "No, that is true, but you did say he is good and kind to you and well what more can you ask of a man but to have his love and trust?"

Rosemary turned her face as a pink tone rushed to her cheeks.

"By the way you talk about him, and how your face shines, I have a feeling you are in love."

Rosemary leaned over to her mom and kissed her on the cheek.

"Oh, and by the way," her mom added, "you did make this pie and I will make sure he knows it. Who knows, maybe he will fall for your apple pie."

The afternoon lagged as Rosemary took her time getting ready. The lavender bubble bath was inviting as she placed the scented soap in the tub. Easing her way into it, she closed her eyes and day dreamed of a place far away where they could be happy with the thought of no random shooting in the streets – a place where a person could walk without fear. The warm water calmed her as she lathered the bubbles up and down her body. The scent was relaxing and she knew that she would smell good when she saw Antonio later that night. Visions of Antonio seemed stuck in her head. She could see his face and hear his voice. The memories of their time together made her pulse rise and she gasped for air. Closing her eyes again, she slowed her breathing down.

What will Mama think of him? She wondered. *Will dad be as easy to persuade like mom was when it came to Antonio not being Italian?*

Meanwhile, Antonio was busy working in the garage with his father finishing up on a car. His eyes swept down to his wrist watch so he could keep track of the time. He did not want to be late for dinner and make a bad impression to her parents on his first visit. How exciting to think he was going to meet them.

"Antonio," John called as he finished an engine on one of Bugs' cars, "you seem very distracted today." Antonio ignored his dad as he shut the hood of the car he was working on. The clinking of tools being thrown in the tool box wiped out his dad's voice. Next he grabbed a rag.

"Done already?" John asked as he was getting up from under the car he was working on.

Antonio gave him a quick glance, and offered a smile. "I'm going to Rosemary's house for dinner tonight."

"Aw," his father said, "to be young and in love again." John's mind traveled back to a time when he first met his wife.

"I remember when I couldn't wait to see your mother. I also remember when I first met her dad," he said crinkling his nose and shaking his head.

"What happened?" Antonio asked curiously while wiping the grease off his hands.

"Well, I think her parents didn't believe I was good enough for her. They gave me the third degree as they questioned me about my family and what I was going to do for a living so I could take care of her. 'She only deserves the best,'" he said in a funny voice to mimic the words of grandpa. He got into the car and started her up. "She sounds good," he said after he turned it off and got out of the car.

Antonio leaned against the work bench. "So what happened? Did they approve?"

"They put up with me," he continued as he grabbed a rag and tried wiping the grease off some of the tools he was using. "You see, your mother and I were in love. We would let nothing stand in our way."

He sighed and his eyes twinkled as he talked about his wife. "Her parents didn't mind that we were going out, but they pushed her to go out with other gentlemen too."

"Did you put up with that?"

"There wasn't much I could do about it. It was the hardest thing I have ever done in my life. To watch the woman I love go out with other man. . But then one day your mother told me she didn't like going out with the other men either and that she was in love with me."

"So, you talked to her dad?"

"Well, I told them I was in love with their daughter, but I think that made things worse for us. So, yes, you can say I tried to talk to them. But they wouldn't listen."

"When did they decide to let you marry her?"

He cocked his head with a silly grin before he answered his son. Taking the clean tools, he threw them into the tool box and let the echo of the sound quit before speaking.

"We were young and impetuous. I talked her into running away with me. She agreed and we eloped." Then he got himself a rag to clean his hands.

"You eloped?" Antonio questioned, moving his body upward away from the bench. His eyebrows lowered onto his nose and a surprised look etched his face. "So how did your relationship carry on with her parents after that?"

"Well, my son, they were not at all pleased with us. But what could they do? We were married. I really thought they were going to disown her forever. It wasn't until your mom became pregnant with you when they really came around." He laughed hitting himself on the thigh. "It is amazing the power of a grandbaby."

"Me?"

"Yes, son, you are the reason they didn't disown us. They were so excited to finally have a grandbaby and well the rest is history." He scratched the back of his neck. "Actually, I think they just put up with me. But I am with the love of my life and didn't let them get in the way."

Antonio walked past his dad and hit him on the back.

"Thanks, dad, for the heads up."

Then he entered the house to take a shower and get ready for whatever might be in store for him at Rosemary's home. He did not know what to expect, but he knew he was in love and nobody was going to keep them apart. Putting on his gray pants, white shirt, and gray vest he looked in the mirror as he combed his hair hoping to make a good first impression.

That evening, the sun was dropping behind the tress as Antonio drove down the street where all the houses mimicked each other, sitting close with only a skinny sidewalk separating them. As he parked the car, he noticed a tall man with an over coat leaving the front door of their home. He tried to focus on the man's face, but his hat seemed to cover his eyes. He wasn't sure if he had seen this man before. He waited for the man to get into his car before he opened the door to get out of his. Walking toward the steps and taking two at a time, he made it to the front door. Nervously, he rang the bell.

Rosemary rushed to the door, opened it, and stepped outside. He took a deep breath as he looked at her. Rosemary was a vision in pink. She wore a form fitting dress adorned with pink and white flowers. It gathered in the middle accentuating her tiny waist, and fell just below her knee. It was enough to take Antonio's breath away. He had an impulse to reach out and touch her face. Instead, he gazed into her eyes. *She's so beautiful,* he thought.

She was surprised how the unexpected thrill still flowed through her as she got close to him. Carefully, he leaned in and kissed her cheek.

"Did you have company?" He asked as his face withdrew from hers.

"No, it was just my cousin," she said without thinking. "Come on in. My dad wants to meet you." Rosemary whispered, as she took his hand and led him into the house. "Try not to be nervous." He knew the interrogation was about to begin. The living room had a couch and a couple of chairs and the box radio on a shelf opposite one of the chairs.

Mike sat in his favorite chair listening to the radio, but stood up and walked to the radio and turned it off when they walked into the room.

"Come on in, Antonio," said Mike in a welcoming tone as he stood by his chair.

Rosemary took a quick breath as she let his hand go.

"Thank you, Sir," Antonio replied respectfully afraid to move. He took in Mikes features, with his big Italian nose, his extended, belly and the gray around his temples.

"Here, have a seat, son," her father offered.

Antonio walked to the chair and gracefully sat down with a straight face and waited for the questions. His eyes were glued to Rosemary. Mike took a chair opposite him and looked him over with squinted eyes.

"Rosemary," shouted Darlene from the dining room, "come and help me set the table." Rosemary shot a questionable look at Antonio before she crept out of the room.

"So, you want to go out with my daughter," Mike said with authority.

"Yes, Sir." Antonio froze in his chair as the man scanned his face.

"You appear to be a nice kid. Rosemary hasn't really said anything to me about you, but she talks to her mother."

Antonio started to squirm in his seat.

"I would never let anything happen to her, Sir," Antonio replied as he wondered what to expect next.

The things his dad had told him haunted his mind. The words of his father *her parents really didn't like me'* echoed in his mind.

"I saw the way my daughter looked at you," Mike continued. "I suspect that she feels the same way about you." He then got up and walked slowly toward the window.

"We're Italian and we watch out for our own, you know?" Mike said with his back to Antonio. "I don't recognize you, boy. Do you go to the same parish as us?"

"Ah, no, Sir."

Mike turned and looked a little more deeply at his features.

"What nationality are you?"

"German- Irish, Sir."

Mike turned to face the window again peering out at the street and any cars that may be traveling down the road.

"I grew up in an Italian neighborhood, and we only mix with our own kind."

Antonio's heart sank deep into his stomach. He tried to prepare himself for this, but to hear the words from Rosemary's father was a discouragement.

"I really thought Rosemary would be asked out by one of those nice boys from church," he said thinking out loud. "I guess this is how it goes in this new world. Women nowadays want an education like my Rosemary. And now they show their legs off in public. I guess I have to get use to the idea that she isn't going to stick with our own kind."

Then his voice grew low as he turned around, eyebrows knit downward to his nose. "You aren't a gangster, are you?"

Antonio noticed how Mike's face turned cold with that statement. "You are not on any

payroll with either Capone or Moran are you?"
He pushed.

With a sound of relief, Antonio
immediately answered, "No, sir. You have no
worries there, Sir." In the back of his mind he
knew not to let this man ever know that even
though he is not on a gangster's payroll, he does
fix up cars for one. But that doesn't make him a
gangster. Why he doesn't even own a gun.

Mike measured his expression for a
moment. Shaking his head with approval, he
walked up to Antonio and stuck out his hand.

Antonio wiped the sweat off his hands
onto his pants as he stood up before shaking
Mike's hand.

"Good," he said as Antonio extended his.
"I don't want my daughter mixed up in that kind
of life."

Mike walked back to his seat, while
Antonio shifted from one foot to the other
wondering what was coming next. When Mike
took his seat Antonio followed, sitting at the
same time.

"Tell me about yourself, son."

Antonio shifted his eyes away for a
moment trying to assemble his thoughts. The
face of Rosemary entered his mind and he
thought of how much she meant to him.

"There isn't much to tell, really," he said
gazing back at Mike while folding his hands on
his lap. "I have six brothers and sisters. My
father owns an automobile mechanic shop and I'm
learning the trade."

"That's good clean work I suppose," Mike
responded nodding his head in approval. "And

you come from a big family, so you know how important family is."

"Oh, yes, Sir. Family is very important to me also. I would like to have a big family someday."

Quietness took over for a few seconds.

"You know this is not an easy town to live in," Mike began shaking his index finger. "Make sure my daughter doesn't get herself in trouble, okay?"

"Of course," squeaked Antonio.

"My little girl has a mind of her own and when she wants something she will go out and get it without thinking of the consequences."

Antonio pursed his lips skeptically before shaking his head. He only knew too well how hard this city was to live in. Thoughts of the shooting at the restaurant entered his mind. He was pretty certain that her parents didn't know about that incident or he would probably not be sitting in their living room right now.

Just then Darlene stepped into the parlor and Antonio jumped to his feet. She seemed surprised to see such manners.

"Hi Antonio," she said walking toward him and reaching out her hand.

"Thank you for inviting me to dinner," he replied graciously as they shook. He thought he may have seen where Rosemary got her eyes.

Her eyes twinkled as she smiled at him and her presence made him feel a little more at ease.

"Come on, child, enough of the interrogation. It's time for dinner," she said looking at both of them with persuading eyes.

Mike sighed deeply and then followed Darlene's lead into the dining room. Antonio waited as Darlene and Mike walked past before he followed them. His nose picked up the wonderful scent of tomatoes and garlic. He glanced at the dining room that looked so pretty with the table set for four. Before he sat down, he glanced at a large china cabinet with beautiful dishes on display. Darlene noticed a look of wonderment on his face.

"Those dishes have very special memories," she said as she walked over and opened the cabinet.

She ever so delicately took out a little china cup. It was white with a silver ring around the middle and at the top of the cup. Inside the cup etching the ridge in teal blue and silver were flowers.

"They have been in my family for over one hundred years. They had belonged to my grandparents, who gave them to my parents, who gave them to me," she said proudly.

He watched her as she caressed the cup before carefully placing it back into the cabinet.

"You can sit here," she said pointing to a chair.

"Thank you, Ma'am."

Antonio waited for Mike and Darlene to sit before he pulled out his chair. He pulled out all his manners for this first meeting. As he was about to sit down, Rosemary walked in with a big bowl of salad. Jumping up he scrambled to her, took the salad from her hands, and set it on the table. Then he pulled out Rosemary's chair before he sat down.

"Thank you," a quiet voice said. She looked up at him, and their eyes locked for a moment before he retreated back to his seat. They didn't noticed how Darlene was taking in all their movements.

"You are welcome," he answered with a smile on his face.

The smell of the food took over and made his mouth water. Darlene gestured to Antonio to start first as they passed around the salad, spaghetti, sauce, and a basket of homemade rolls. Except for the mumblings of please and thank you as the food was being passed around, everyone was quiet. It was not until a couple of bites had been taken that the silence was broken.

"This is really good," Antonio said as he took another bite full of spaghetti.

"Thank you," said Darlene blushing. She neatly used a spoon to twirl her fork with spaghetti. "I always say that the way to a man's heart is through his stomach," she mused. Mike shot her a look.

Rosemary grimaced as Antonio shot a playful glance at her. Sounds of forks scrapping the plates were in the background.

"Well, if she can cook this good, I'm hooked," Antonio laughed before he took another bite. He took another fork full of spaghetti as Rosemary shot him another dirty look. Mike grabbed a roll to help wipe up the sauce on his plate.

"Wait till you see what's for dessert," bragged Darlene between bites. "Rosemary baked it herself."

Rosemary felt her face become warm with embarrassment.

"You made the desert?" Antonio asked excitedly. "You never told me you can cook. I would have been over sooner if I knew you were cooking."

"Well, Sir, I am a school girl and cooking is not my forte at the moment."

"You heard what your mother said. The way to a man's heart is through his stomach."

"But I am not looking for a man's heart," she declared.

"And what is for dessert?" He played along.

Darlene picked up the platter of spaghetti and passed it toward Antonio with a nod. "More?" He gladly took the platter from her hands.

"Antonio, this girl can cook very well. I don't understand why she wastes her time going to school. She is at the age to find a nice young man," she paused and glanced quickly at Antonio who seemed to be enjoying his meal. "and get married and make babies."

Darlene kept her eyes on him, noticing how Antonio and Rosemary shared a loving glance. That made her smile to herself.

Mike looked at Darlene and gave her a stern glare. "Don't push, Darlene," was all he said.

"I think Rosemary should do whatever she wants to do," Antonio cut in causing her to blush this time.

"Thank you, kind Sir," she said sarcastically.

Rosemary took a piece of bread and sopped up the sauce on her plate before putting it in her mouth. Her ideals with relation to her future had changed since she met Antonio. School used to be her main focus, but all she could do at that point was think about him. She placed her elbows on the table and rested her chin on her hands as she watched Antonio enjoy his food. Her future still consisted of being a teacher and helping children, but she also wanted Antonio in the picture.

"Rosemary," gestured her mother to get her attention, "let's clear the table so we can have some dessert."

Quickly, she took the last bite from her plate before she stood up and helped her mother remove the dirty dishes. Silence filled the dining room as the men waited for the women to return. Neither man looked at each other. Walking back into the dining room, the girls each had two plates of hot apple pie. The smell was overwhelming and made Antonio's mouth water. Mike peered up at Darlene and smiled.

"You know what this reminds me of, dear?" He asked taking a plate from her.

"Yes, I do," she replied taking her seat. "How we met."

She looked up at her husband and smiled lovingly. It was not difficult to see the strong bond they still had for each other.

"So how did you meet?" Antonio asked trying to ease back into a conversation with Mike.

Darlene and Rosemary shared a quick glance as they waited for Mike to speak. He took another bite of pie, swallowed, and then cleared his throat.

"We were young and she worked in the kitchen at church. She looked so lovely making apple pies." He turned his head and cast his eyes upon his wife. "She's still as lovely today, if not more as when we first met."

Not a word was said for a few seconds as they exchanged another loving glance that made Darlene blush. Rosemary knew at that moment that she wanted what her parents had together.

"I asked her if I could help, but she pushed me out of the kitchen," he continued with a big smile showing all of his teeth. "I think she was playing hard to get... But I still managed to get her phone number so that I could call her for a date."

Rosemary's eye quickly shifted toward her mother as she listened to her father's version of the story. A warm smile came over Darlene's face before she spoke.

"That's not quite how we met, dear. I think you're having trouble with your memory."

He studied her face and chuckled.

"Don't you remember coming back into the kitchen and helping me with the dishes? That was the first kind thing you did for me when we met. How could I not let you take me out?"

"Are you sure about that?" he shrugged. "You are still as pretty now as the first time we met," he said softly.

They both reached across the table and touched fingers. The rest of the dinner talk seemed comfortable, mostly centered on Rosemary's school and the kind of cars Antonio fixed. Antonio was very careful not to name the person that some of the cars belonged to. The laughter, company and food made for a special night. But time got away from them and it was soon time for Antonio to leave.

Standing up Antonio helped clear the dessert dishes from the dinner table and put them in the kitchen sink. Darlene was running the water in the sink to wash the dishes.

"Can I help you?" Asked Antonio as he set the dirty plates next to the sink.

'No thank you, dear," she said as Mike strolled into the kitchen. "I already have help. Here take this towel to dry the dishes," she motioned to Mike.

"Thank you for a wonderful meal," Antonio said as he reached out to shake Darlene's hand. She gave him a hug.

"Don't be a stranger," was all she said.

Then he turned to Mike and they shook hands as he thanked him also.

Rosemary was leaning against the archway, with her arms crossed, between the kitchen and dining room waiting for him. He walked up to her saying ladies first and followed her to the front door. He opened the door and they stepped outside. He put his hand lightly around her waist and pulled her close.

With his other hand, he traced her cheek from her ear to her chin. Staring into her eyes, he reluctantly let her go, but not until he placed a soft kiss on her lips and told her good night.

"Till tomorrow, my sweet," he said.

Chapter Nine

Love Grows; Revenge Prevails

Over the next couple of months, their love bloomed. They met regularly at the coffee shop each morning before Rosemary went to school. Antonio always sat with two cups in front of him and waited patiently. When the door opened and as he saw the familiar figure walk in, he sighed. Then he stood up and pulled out a chair for her.

After saying, "Thank you," she sat down.

Antonio closed his eyes to take in the sweet scent of her perfume. Rosemary wrapped her hands around her cup, the edges of her mouth curled up as she gazed into his eyes.

"I love starting my day with you," Antonio admitted.

Rosemary blushed as she listened to words that she wanted to hear.

"I love starting my days this way too," she said softly.

Using her fingers, she twisted her hair. He took a deep breath as he watched her and thought of a hundred ways, he could lure her from school just to be alone with her again.

Every morning started this way before ending up with her in school and him learning more about car mechanics from his father. After school, he would be there to pick her up and they would decide what to do. Sometimes they spent a few hours at his garage where Antonio would show off his new skills.

"How would you like to ride around in this beauty?" He said one day as he opened the door of a new sedan. Rosemary stroked the cold, smooth, black vehicle as she walked around it. She loved to see the excitement on his face as he sat in the driver's side getting comfortable and pretending, he owned it.

"Has Antonio showed you how he fixed this car?" John asked as he opened the hood.

"I hear he had a good teacher," Rosemary replied playfully as she showed interest in the engine.

On some days, they spent a few hours at Rosemary's house either helping to make a meal or with Antonio bothering her while she tried to study.

"Here's the potato peeler," Rosemary said while she washed the potatoes.

"Hey, cooking is girls' work," Antonio teased.

He pressed his lips together and stared at her through narrow eyes. His eyes then flashed down to the potato peeler and back to her. He enjoyed watching her and his gaze followed her while she finished washing the potatoes and brought the bowl to the table. She made a face as she showed Antonio how to peel them.

Darlene eventually walked into the kitchen and scooted the two of them out into the living room so she could finish the dinner preparations herself.

"Go, child," she said taking the peeler from her hands. "Enjoy your company."

Rosemary gave her mother a quick hug. Then picking up her books, she and Antonio entered the living room. Settling on the couch, she pulled out her literature book and began to read. Antonio made himself comfortable, slowly lying on the couch and putting his head in her lap. Smiling blissfully up at Rosemary, he gazed unrelentingly into her eyes. He slowly moved her book to the side so she had to look at him. She was still trying to read, but the words became blurry. He seemed to hypnotize her. He caressed her cheek and their eyes held with flickers of electricity charging the atmosphere. With his fingers tangled in her hair, he drew her head downward while bringing his face up until his lips brushed against hers. It was a soft kiss that lingered for only a moment, but his gaze locked on her angelic face.

On weekends, they enjoyed getting away to go for walks to the ice cream parlor, or sit at the coffee shop and talk. They became inseparable, fingers always intertwined when they walked, and their days mingled with moments of passion as they tasted each other's lips.

***

The war was still raging between Al Capone and George 'Bugs' Moran. Frank and Pete, the Gusenberg brothers, had their final meeting with Bugs on how to get rid of Al's advisor, Pasqualino 'Patsy' Lolordo.

"So it will happen today," stated Frank with a proud tone to his voice as he walked towards the bar. "We found a friend of Pasqualino who does not know who we are, but we assured him we needed to do some business with him. He has planned a time for us to visit with Pasqualino." Pete and Frank each got a glass of whiskey and sat down.

George walked around the room shaking his head while listening to the voice of his gang brother. "Are you sure this won't be a trap?"

"It better not be," the questionable voice of Pete answered almost spitting out his drink. "That means we will die and I am not prepared to die today." His eyes shot up to Frank.

"I told you, I have this covered, Pete."

"Can you trust this man?" Asked George. "I don't want to lose my two best men either." He stopped walking letting his eyes focus on Frank.

"Yes, we can trust him," the perturbed voice answered.

"How can you be so sure?" Asked Pete.

Frank rolled his eyes and took another sip of his drink. He swallowed before finally answering him. He glanced at Pete before letting his eyes roll to George. "I told them; I knew of a way to destroy George 'Bugs' Moran." He took a deep breath, and kept a steady eye on his boss. He wasn't really sure how 'Bugs' was going to take this. "This man was delighted to see me."

The room was quiet. The sound of George footsteps echoed in the small space. Finally the man stopped and laughed out loud.

"I love it!" He boomed.

That night with the help of this friend, Pete and Frank they made their way into Pasqualino's home. The friend knocked on the door and introduced Patsy to Pete and Frank. While Patsy's wife made dinner in the kitchen, Patsy voluntarily let these men inside. The friend said goodbye and when the door was shut, they waited for a few minutes to make sure the friend was far enough away before they took out their guns and assassinated Patsy in his own living room. When his wife heard the shots, she ran out of the kitchen and found her husband lying in a pool of blood. As she knelt down beside him and cried for the loss of her husband, the two men let themselves out.

Meanwhile, Al was hosting a party when he heard the news of his good friend's death. He went into mourning after the murder and his hatred for Bugs grew ever stronger.

Chapter Ten

Heartbreak

Rosemary and Antonio carried out their morning ritual before going their separate ways for the day. Rosemary went to her classes and Antonio to fix cars in his father's garage. That morning, Bugs walked into the garage as Antonio finished cleaning another carburetor. His guard was down and although he knew Bugs was the head of the North side gang, he considered him just as a nice customer.

"Boy, is this a pretty car," Antonio said in a matter of fact tone.

As he washed grease from his hands, he admired the sleek curves of the fenders on the 1927 Rolls Royce. He also noted how smooth and shiny the body appeared.

"Yeah, she's a real beauty, isn't she?" Bugs stated as Antonio cleaned the mirrors with a rag.

Watching this young man's enthusiasm, Bugs thought back to his younger days and the excitement he felt when he was near a beautiful car.

"Want to go for a ride?" He asked.

Antonio's eyes flashed up with an eager expression on his face.

"Really?" Came out of his mouth without thinking.

Even in the excitement of the moment with the possibility of driving this beautiful car, Antonio pictured himself shielding Rosemary from bullets that flew through the air from Bugs' boys. At least that's what the paper said. He hated the fact that this man – a gangster – a lead player – made Chicago such a dangerous place to live in. However, being an auto mechanic, he loved cars, especially beautiful ones like this Rolls. Controversy played with his mind as he continued to admire the vehicle.

"Come on," Bugs urged as he slid into the passenger seat. "I have a little time to kill."

Antonio hesitated for just a moment before hopping into the driver's seat and wiggling until he felt comfortable. His pulse rose with anticipation. He put his hands on the wheel and let his fingers caress it for a moment before starting up the engine. Listening to the sweet-sounding purr of the engine, he put it into gear and slowly drove out of the garage. Bugs watched him with amusement.

"Go on," he smiled wistfully, "give it some gas."

With a turn of his head and a quick glance at the man, Antonio shot a mysterious smile before he shifted into a higher gear. Bugs turned on the radio while Antonio drove. He felt like royalty as he steered the beautiful car down the street paying no attention to the heads turning in his direction or the passing cars that slowed down for a better look.

"This vehicle is great!" Antonio said.

He carefully maneuvered the car, while the wind soared through the open window ruffled his hair. He felt exceptionally excited and glad to be alive. Watching the buildings fly past with the wind hitting his face, he felt as if he were on top of the world. Bugs enjoyed the priceless look on Antonio's face while being driven around.

Mike was checking the sign outside of his store when he noticed the Rolls Royce pull up at the stoplight. He stood in awe as he looked at the sleek black body, which sparkled as the sun's rays danced upon it. His eyes traced around the body of the car and then he noticed the driver. Smiling to himself, he was about to call out a name, but then the car turned the corner and he recognized Bugs in the passenger side. His eyes grew big with hatred as he stood in one spot staring. His arms stiffened and his hands clenched into fists. He glared at the car as it drove away.

It couldn't be, he thought and walked back inside the store with hate-filled eyes.

"Darlene!" He yelled hastily standing by the counter.

"What's all the yelling about?" Asked Darlene as she strolled out of the back room. As she made it to the front of the store, she found Mike with his back stiffened and eyes enraged.

"What do you know about this Antonio?" He questioned. Fear passed through him like a dark flame.

His rough voice and the expression on his face scared her, as the hairs on her arms stood up. "He's Rosemary's boyfriend," she responded hugging her body. "He's a good boy. He's kind to her and I think they're in love."

Mike raised his fist in the air and slammed it down on the counter top. A jar of gumballs fell on its side and gumballs bounced to the floor.

"He comes over all the time. You know he's a good boy, Mike," she repeated frightened by his reaction.

"No!" He hollered, his face reddening with anger. "We will have no part of him in our home anymore."

" W-W-Why?" She struggled to ask.

Mike started talking quickly in Italian. A lui è piaciuto - egli è un gangster - lavora per i Bug Moran. His arms moved as fast as his lips. His face burned with pure anger and his eyes narrowed. Darlene stood in silence waiting for him to calm down. She had not seen him this angry in years and it truly scared her.

"Calm down," she insisted. "Remember what the doctor said about your blood pressure." She paused to take a breath. "Now what are you talking about? Why can't Antonio come around anymore?" She asked with control in her voice.

"He lied," he said switching to English.

"What did he lie about?" She asked, confused. Her jaw dropped as her eye brows raised.

"I saw him," he said quickly and dryly. "I saw him. That's all that matters."

"Slow down, Mike. I don't understand."

Mike paced back and forth, deliberately putting one foot in front of the other in a constant rhythm, in front of the counter. His eyebrows burrowed over his nose, not listening to his wife, the vision of Antonio in the beautiful Rolls Royce with Bugs as the passenger of that car infuriated him.

"What are you talking about?" She insisted staring at him intently.

"I'm sorry, Darlene," he grimaced, "but he's not allowed in our home ever again."

He continued to stare at her with an 'in charge' look about him. She knew there was no changing his mind when he got like that, but she had to try.

"Well, that doesn't seem fair, does it?" She challenged him.

Mike stopped abruptly and shrugged his shoulders.

"It doesn't seem fair that he didn't tell us who he works for..." he paused for a moment. His voice rose louder as he finished his sentence. "Moran!" The stress of it all had the veins in his forehead popping out. "He told me he was a good boy. He told me he wasn't a gangster."

Mike resumed his pacing again swinging his arms up and down. Tears filled Darlene's eyes as she stared blankly at him frozen in place. She took a deep breath before she spoke.

"You could be mistaken, Mike," she said trying not to believe what she heard. Her mind tried to take in all that he said. It just did not make sense to her.

"He was driving Moran around in this big, fancy car," he said sarcastically, his hands still clenched in fists. "Why would he be driving Moran around, if he wasn't one of his boys? How could Antonio lie to me and I didn't see it?" He said pacing in circles around the store.

Darlene knelt down with the jar and picked up the fallen gumballs. The idea of Rosemary going out with someone from one of the gangs frightened her to no end. She envisioned the two kids in her front room and how happy her daughter was when Antonio came over. But to hang around with one of Moran's boys was a frightening thought. Mike was Al's cousin and Bugs Moran was the enemy. Al helped Mike get his little corner store and kept Moran's boys from bothering them.

What if Al saw Rosemary being driven around town with one of Moran's boys? She worried.

That thought unnerved Mike too and he became weak in the knees. He grabbed onto the counter, his face pale and moist with sweat. Darlene ran to his side and grabbed a chair as he slumped against the wall to catch his fall.

"What's wrong?" She asked.

She took a towel and wiped his forehead. He opened his mouth, but nothing came out. He held his right hand to his chest, while closing his eyes trying to slow down his breathing. Darlene started to panic. Gently, she took his hand in hers and stared at his face to get his attention. Slowly, he opened his eyes and gazed into her beautiful brown eyes, which penetrated his. Then her lips curled up forming a little smile. She squeezed his hand and the lines by her eyes increased. This was the angel he married so many years ago.

"Slow down your breathing," was all she said. He kept his eyes on her and tried to follow her instructions.

"She is not to meet with him anymore. Yes?" He finally gasped.

Darlene knelt down to his level never letting her eyes leave his face. They stared at each other sharing a frightened expression.

"Yes," she agreed. "We will tell her tonight."

Al was walking around the corner when he noticed the Rolls Royce pull up at the stoplight. Of course, the beautiful car made him take a second look, but it was the driver that caught his eye. He starred at the driver wondering where he saw him before. As he went through the files in his head, the car turned and he saw George Moran. At that same moment the file with the face came to his mind. Wasn't that the boy Rosemary was with at the restaurant?

Meanwhile, school was finally out and Antonio was waiting as usual. Rosemary skipped to the car while her heart leapt. He waited for her wearing a huge smile.

"This is the best part of my day," he said taking her books from her and putting them into the car. He swung his arm around her waist and drew her near as his eyes searched her face. Then he let his lips gently kiss hers. Rosemary gladly moved in for the kiss, her arms flung around his neck to pull him closer. Her hands explored his head with her fingers knotted in his hair. He slowly let her lips go still kissing around her cheeks and neck as he listened to her fast and hard breath. Smiling to himself, he released her and helped her into the car. She watched with anticipation as he walked around the car and got in. She scooted close to him and brought her face near his before she softly kissed his neck.

"Hold on, tiger," he chuckled as he started up the car. "What are the plans for tonight?"

Disappointed, she stopped kissing him and frowned.

"I have a test in my science class tomorrow so I need to study tonight," she muttered. "I will miss you, but I will dream of you."

He looked into her eyes dazed by her beauty. "I will dream of you too, my love."

He drove her to her home as they held hands with fingers interlocked. He parked the car before he pulled her close and took in her scent. He let his lips kiss her on the forehead and then her cheek, before kissing her lips. She felt his lips on her face and quivered with his touch. When his lips touched her lips, her body shivered and her mouth opened to receive him.

"I have to go," she whispered in between the kisses. He slowly let her go, both of them breathing heavy.

"I love you," he panted before he released her. He got out and opened the car door for her. Jumping back in, he waited until she stepped inside before he drove off.

Darlene and Mike sat in the living room waiting for Rosemary to arrive. As the car pulled up and they glanced outside to see Antonio jump out and opened the door for their daughter. After giving him a quick kiss, they got away from the window.

"Mama, Papa," she said with surprise as she entered the house.

She ran up to them giving each of them a hug. She immediately noticed the stiffness in their bodies.

"What's wrong?" She asked somewhat alarmed. They looked like someone had died.

Her eyes went from her mother's face to her father's expressionless look.

"Well?" She pushed and stood waiting for an answer.

"Sit down," said her father in a low, but harsh voice.

As she walked to the couch, he started pacing the floor. The tone of his voice scared her along with his pacing, so she automatically obeyed.

"What's wrong?" Rosemary asked sitting down on the couch.

She rubbed her hands on her lap and watched her father – still pacing – shaking his head, mouth open wanting to say something, but then closing it. Suddenly, his hands flew up in the air, waving wildly and he went into another rant in Italian. A lui è piaciuto – egli è un gangster – lavora per i Bug Moran. Her mother sat quietly keeping her concerned eyes on him.

Rosemary was dumbfounded. *Why is he acting this way?* She wondered.

"Mike," said Darlene breaking the silence, "your heart. Stay calm and just talk." Rosemary glanced quickly at her mother, but her mother would not let their eyes meet.

"You will not see Antonio anymore!" Mike shouted. The harshness of his voice and his words made Rosemary jump.

Walking toward the couch he waved a finger in her face and added, "Do you understand?"

Rosemary stared at his creased eyebrows and angry face.

"What?" She asked, her body tense. "I am not a child anymore. You can't tell me who I can and can't see." She surprised herself with the tone and response she gave her father. She had never been disrespectful before.

"I said you will not see him anymore," he scowled.

"What are you talking about?" Rosemary asked as tears formed in her eyes. "He is kind and you have seen how nice he is?"

Her body began to shake with fear. Her pulse was jumping at an accelerated rate and it was not because she was in love. This was fear, almost like the fear she experienced in the restaurant shooting, or maybe even worse.

"He's a gangster and I will not have a daughter of mine being part of a gang," he said. Rosemary's mouth dropped open. Her arms went up in the air with her fingers extended.

"He isn't a gangster," she pleaded. The fear of never seeing him again made her quiver.

How could her father think this kind and gracious man was a gangster? Why would her father think that she would even go out with someone like that? He knows how she feels about her cousin Al and how she hates the way the man lives. Should she tell him about how Antonio saved her when she was at the restaurant where someone tried to kill her cousin? How he put his life before hers. But then maybe that would not be a good idea either.

"What are you talking about?" She glanced at her mother looking for support, but she kept her eyes down.

"I recognized him," her father continued.

Rosemary's eyes flashed back to him. She opened her mouth to talk, but he stopped her.

"I saw him and I will not allow this." He paused to flash her, a hard look. "I will not allow you to live that kind of life."

Tears escaped from her eyes and started running down Rosemary's face as she listened. *Why is he so mad? Why does he think Antonio is a gangster,* she wondered? It was getting hard for her to breathe because she was choking on the tears in the back of her throat.

"What did Antonio do?" She finally managed to get out.

Her memories of him were only good ones with shared kissed and the way he protected her from the shooting at the restaurant. Without thinking, she said the next thing on her mind.

"I love him," she blurted out in between breaths as her eyes pleaded with her father.

She paused knowing what she just said changed everything. Without thinking, Mike marched over to his daughter, his hand flying in the air. She felt the sting on her face as he drew his hand away. Darlene jumped from her seat and ran over to her daughter. Rosemary sat still, tears falling from her eyes, her hands clutched over her cheek where the pain was just inflicted, crying loud and hard. Her hands trembled as her breath quickened.

"Why?" Was all she managed to utter.

Her father glared angrily into his daughter's eyes. She never felt such fright as she did at that moment. Her mother sat and rocked her while her father sat in his chair and dropped his head into his hands. Rosemary was terrified and not sure she wanted to hear what he had to say.

"Rosemary," he finally said as he raised his face, in a controlled tone. "I saw Antonio in a Rolls Royce with Bugs Moran."

Rosemary's eyes widened as her breaths became ragged and harsh. This must all be a big mistake. Her head shaking quickly back and forth with quiet, "No's," coming from her mouth.

"It's dangerous for you to be seen with him," he continued. "Remember, Al Capone is my cousin. You also know how he takes care of this family."

Rosemary gasped for air as her tears continued to flow. *This can't be true,* she thought.

They spent so much time together, both at her home and at his father's garage. She had never seen Bugs and his name never came up in conversation. There had to be some kind of mistake. This man told her he wanted to take her out of this gangster town.

"You will not have anything more to do with him," her father repeated, his jaw hardened. "Do you understand?"

Rosemary listened, trying to make sense of it all. The room seemed to be closing in on her making it hard to breathe. Her eyes were blurry from all the tears and the sound of her heart beating so loud was making it even more difficult to hear her father talk. This could not be happening.

"Promise," her dad continued.

Both of her parents stared at her waiting for an answer. *Did her dad really see him in a car with Bugs Moran? Was he that good to be able to keep such a big secret away from her? Why did he steal her heart if only to break it by the one thing she told him from the beginning she didn't want anything to do with? What else can I do,* she wondered and nodded glumly.

Mike stood up and walked toward his daughter. With his hand he reached down toward her face and lightly brushed her sore cheek. "Sorry," he whispered.

Rosemary excused herself and rushed to her room. Running inside and slamming the door, she fell on her bed sobbing.

Could he really be one of Moran's boys? She considered. *He's so kind and gentle, and we talked about leaving this town. Is that why he wants to leave so badly? What if Al recognized him at the restaurant where the shooting took place? Would he have shot Antonio?*

She pictured him in her mind, the curve of his face, the way he'd lightly touch her lips with his.

That's not the way a killer would act, she thought. *They have to be mistaken... but what if they're right? What if we are seen together by the wrong people?*

Rosemary's head started to throb. This was way too complicated to think about. Yet her heart ached for him. Her mind stayed preoccupied with thoughts of the conversation with her parents.

Maybe a bath would make her feel better. She stepped in the tub but instead of a bath she let the water run. She stood in the shower letting the water flow over her head, into her eyes, and all over her body. She hoped the magic of the steaming water would relax her, but instead she just cried. The tension of the moment took over and she sobbed irrepressibly until she found herself sitting in the bathtub under the still running shower. She cried and cried until she noticed the water had turned cold.

She stepped out and dried off. As she looked into the steamed mirror, her reflection revealed bloodshot and puffy eyes. Quickly she put on a pair of pajamas and lay back in the bed. The tears did not stop until finally she fell asleep totally exhausted completely missing dinner.

It was late evening when she awoke. She thought she heard voices coming from downstairs so she silently crept to the top of the stairs.

"I can't believe it," she heard Al say as he sat in the living room talking with her father.

"I'm sorry, Al," Mike replied.

"Thanks for having me over for dinner," Al continued. "I just needed family to talk to." His voice sounded broken up as he rattled on. "Patsy was a good friend. Why would anyone go into his home to kill him?"

Mike sat listening and shaking his head.

"It's that no good Bugs Moran. He went into his home. I can't believe he would stoop so low."

Al stood up, made a fist in his right hand, and slammed the palm of his left hand. "He will have to pay!" He hollered.

Observing his cousin's behavior, even Mike became unnerved. Darlene walked into the living room and toward Al. He heard her coming and sat down again with tears in his eyes. Feeling for him, she cuddled him like a child putting his head on her chest.

"Now, now, Al" she said. "I don't know why you chose this kind of life."

He slowly moved his head away and peered at her with tears in his eyes. He was always careful not to talk shop around the women. However, he knew she wasn't blind to what was happening. She read the paper and was married to his cousin. Who knows what Mike might have told her?

"It would not matter what kind of life I lived," he said. "A lot of innocent people have died at the hands of Moran's men just for being at the wrong place at the wrong time."

Darlene felt the hair rise on her arms as that statement came from his mouth with a passing thought of Rosemary and Antonio. Mike glanced up at Darlene with a frightened look that they both shared.

"Thanks for being here for me," Al said slowly rising from the couch. "I'll let you know when the funeral will be held."

He leaned down and gave Darlene a swift kiss goodbye. Mike walked with him to the door and gave him a hug.

Rosemary could not keep her feelings bottled in any longer and ran down the stairs, rushing past her mother, whisking her father out of the way, and stopped in door way where Al was. Her eyes glared hatred at the man as he tuned to see her.

"It is all because of you," she cried as she started hitting him in the chest. The tears rolled down her cheeks and her fists didn't stop hitting the man until he held her close. "It is all because of you that I can't be with the man I love."

Darlene ran to the front door, while Mike tried to stop Rosemary from hitting Al. Al just looked at them and nodded his head to let them know he had this handled. He shut the front door giving them some privacy from her parents. They stood on the front porch, as he held her tight, not really sure what she was talking about and didn't let her go until he could feel her body start to relax.

"I don't understand," was all he said as he loosened his grip. He put his hands on her shoulders and pulled her back just enough to look at her face. Tears streaked her cheeks. "Do you know who I saw today?" Not giving her time to answer he went on. "I saw your boyfriend driving George Moran around in a Rolls Royce." His voice started to choke. "This is the same man who went into my friend's house and killed him in his living room."

Another tear slipped down her cheek. She yanked her arms away from him as she took jagged breaths.

"Rosemary you have bad taste in men." His voice was in a low growl. "I better not see him around you anymore." Then to her surprise he added, "I am afraid for your life. Don't you understand? That is why he killed Patsy. It was to get to me."

"Antonio would n-n-never h-h-hurt me," she stuttered in between tears.

"Maybe not, but that won't stop Moran from coming here to kill you just to try and get to me." She froze in place as a couple more tears escaped from her eyes.

Rosemary stared at him taking it all in and then suddenly she turned away from him and opened the front door. She walked past her parents and back up the stairs.

"What was that about?" Mike asked Al, his eyes searching Al's face for the answer.

"I don't know," he said in a sad tone keeping their conversation private. He shook his head and turned to leave.

"Night," they said in unison before Mike closed the door.

When Mike turned around, he saw Darlene wringing her hands. She was as white as a ghost and trembling. She glanced up at him. "I'm scared for Rosemary," she said.

Mike studied her face as he walked up to her and pulled her close. She needed his strength at that moment. She put her head on his shoulder and wrapped her arms tightly around him.

"She'll be all right as long as we can keep an eye on her," he whispered. A couple more tears fell from Darlene's eyes.

Rosemary stormed back into her room and fell on her bed, tears bubbling over once again. She hated to see her parents so scared and it hurt her to see her mother cry. The earlier conversation rolled around in her mind.

Why somebody would walk into Dean's home and kill him? She wondered. *Did I hear him right?*

Shivers ran down her arms causing her to jump under the covers for warmth. She tried not to think. What she most needed was sleep, but the day had been far too eventful. She rolled on her side and drew her knees up to her chest. She never even got to study for her test, but she had to sleep. She closed her eyes, but conversations kept intruding into her mind. The words that she could not see Antonio anymore echoed over and over. Al's account of the shooting of his friend also stayed in her head. It was not until she pictured Antonio's face and heard his voice tell her he loved her that she finally drifted off.

It was a bright sunny day as Rosemary strolled down a busy Chicago street. She walked up to the ice cream store when she noticed Antonio waiting for her. He stuck out his hand and she took it before they walked inside. He ordered a couple of cones – one vanilla and one chocolate. After he paid for them, he handed her the chocolate one.

Once outside, she took a lick of her ice cream and he asked if he could taste the flavor she had. When she answered 'yes,' he held her close, kissed her, and told her how good it tasted. She never thought she could be so happy. After he released her, a loud metallic sound entered her ears. Antonio fell to the ground and Al walked up with a gun in his hand and a stern look on his face.

"Stay away from my family," he said firmly.

Rosemary awoke screaming in her bed. She was trembling and her body was moist with perspiration. Looking around, she realized that it was only a dream – a very bad dream. Taking a deep breath, she rolled over and tried to fall asleep again.

Chapter Eleven

Love Conquers All

Waking up to the sunshine in her bedroom and looking at her clock, Rosemary rushed to get ready for school. Her face was swollen from all the crying she had done the night before, so she tried to mask it with make-up. Her parents had already left for work, so the house was quiet like usual. She barely made the bus on time and there was no room to sit, but she didn't care. She stood there hanging on to the pole with people bumping her as they either got on or off the bus, but her mind was a million miles away.

Running late, she avoided the coffee shop. As she approached school, the familiar car with the face of the man she loved was waiting for her. Tears welled in her eyes as she ignored him and walking swiftly up to the steps towards the front of the school without looking in his direction. The possibility of being seen with him was too dangerous. Antonio scanned everyone who passed the coffee shop. Anxiously, he had waited for her and it was getting late.

"Rosemary," Antonio called as he caught a glimpse of her running up ahead. She didn't turn her head, or glance back.

"Rosemary," he called again as she ran into the building. She didn't acknowledge him, leaving him utterly confused. He angrily slammed the car door before he sped home.

Rosemary refused to dwell on thoughts of him, while her science test kept her mind busy. The test took a little longer and was harder than she expected, but she reminded herself that she did not have a chance to study. As soon as she finished her test, thoughts of him rushed in again.

How can our relationship go on, if it's not safe to be around him? She wondered.

Now more than ever, she wanted to get out of Chicago.

School seemed to go by slowly that morning as she tried to concentrate on her schoolwork. However, thoughts of Antonio kept interrupting them. At noon she decided to eat in the cafeteria rather than go outside just in case he was waiting for her. She was not only confused by the fact that he might not have been truthful with her, but she was also afraid for her life.

Would Al shoot both of us, if he saw us together, she pondered? The words of her cousin echoed in her mind. *'I saw your boyfriend driving George Moran around in a Rolls Royce. This is the same man who went into my friend's house and killed him in his living room. Rosemary you have bad taste in men. I better not see him around you anymore.'*

When the school day ended, Rosemary walked briskly toward the exit door, but without enthusiasm. She did not want to face

Antonio – not yet. She peered outside and sure enough, there he stood beside his car. She managed to mingle in a crowd and escaped without him spotting her.

"Dinner will be ready soon, Rosemary!" Shouted her mother from the kitchen.

Rosemary ran upstairs and tried to concentrate on her homework. Her mind spiraled out of control, fluctuating between Antonio being in Bug's group and her loving boyfriend. Her body shook with fear, her chest hurt, and she wondered if she could really keep her promise to her parents. She had to talk to him one more time. She needed to hear him actually say he was one of the gang to make it easier to live without him. And her fear of living without Antonio dominated her more than Capone's men ever could. She was not sure she could cut him out of her life that easily. Her head ached as she waited for the day to end so she could sleep and not have to think anymore.

Meanwhile, Antonio could not figure out what was happening.

Why did Rosemary ignore me? He wondered. *What did I do wrong?*

It was the first time since they started seeing each other that she ditched him – harshly and unexpectedly. The tires squealed as he accelerated quickly on his way to Rosemary's house. He walked up to the front door and rang the bell.

"Hi, Mike," he said nonchalantly. "Is Rosemary home?"

Mike stared at Antonio without smiling. Antonio could feel the new dislike from this man and had no understanding as to why.

"She doesn't want to see you anymore," he said coldly.

Antonio shifted from one foot to the other with his eyes glued on the man talking to him. He could tell that something had changed and he was no longer invited into this house.

Mike's hand never left the doorknob and it was turning white as he squeezed it tightly. "Don't ever come around here again," he demanded before closing the door.

Antonio stood dazed and confused. The words rang through his head, *'She doesn't want to see you anymore.'* He had to have answers. Mike's words exploded in his mind and his face turned bright red. He tried to keep his anger under control.

He knocked on the door again, but no one answered. Getting more upset, he knocked again and again. Eventually, Mike opened the door with a hard expression on his face.

"Go home and don't ever come back here, young man!" He barked, before slamming the door shut.

Antonio's pulse raced as he quickly jumped into his car. His foot hit the accelerator speeding home, blowing through a stop sign. Another car honked and he veered out of the way. His mind was not on the road; rather it was on the days he spent with Rosemary. He tried to relive each one mentally. He blew another stop narrowly missing a car that was crossing in front of him. He knew he should slow down, but his emotions had gotten the better of him. He had to figure out what he had done to upset her. He pictured her face. Her beautiful eyes that had dazed him from the beginning. He could not picture himself living without her.

He went to bed shortly after arriving home, but didn't sleep well and woke up exhausted. He showered and left the house straight to the coffee shop. He needed answers, and if that meant he kept her from her morning classes then so be it. He had to know if what her father had said was true. Time passed and like the day before, she didn't show up.

To help alleviate his frustration, he drove back to the garage to work. He decided to check on her again the following day.

Rosemary got off the bus and mingled with a group of students so Antonio wouldn't spot her. She thought she noticed his car, so she kept her head low and blended into the middle of the crowd. She made it to the building without a confrontation. She did it again, another day without him. However, the day went by slowly as she thought about him and the answers, she needed plagued her mind. She was in her math class and then her history class to follow each of her classes seemed to drag. She was keeping her promise to her parents, but the question remained: how long would she be able to hold her ground. What kind of a hold did he have on her? She was in love and this just didn't make any sense. She needed answers, but was not sure how to get them.

Another day passed, but this time Antonio changed his strategy. He parked his car outside of the school and quickly went in looking for her. Walking inside, he looked around at the people passing by him. The noise of laughter and talking overtook his senses making him more upset. With his pulse bounding, he decided to wait inside close to the wall where he had full view of the doorway. He watched as students walked in talking or drinking their coffee before class. It was getting late and as fewer people came by, he became worried that Rosemary might not even show up for her classes. *Was she all right? Was she sick?* He knew how important school was to her. His mind ran in so many directions that he had trouble concentrating. He had to find her. He had to talk to her and let her know what she meant to him.

Rosemary had been in the middle of a group of students when she walked in and noticed Antonio in the hallway. She knew he had not seen her, but her heart ached as she looked upon him.

He's so handsome but he looks so confused, she thought. Her pulse was rapid again just with him in sight. She found it hard to breath. She tried to convince herself that there was no way her father or Al saw him in George's car, driving him around. But why would her father lie to her? She wanted to go up to him, hold him tight, and tell him everything was all right, but she couldn't. She had to know who he really was and if he had been lying to her all this time just to steal her heart. The real question was how to talk to him again without accusing him of anything. She took her hand and tried to rub the pain that was beginning in her temple.

Her mind fought between the promise she made to her parents and how much she missed him. Without permission her legs strolled towards him breaking her promise to her parents.

"Hello," said a soft voice behind Antonio.

He turned quickly to the sound of her voice. He smiled slightly, but his eyes were hard.

"Where have you been?" He asked keeping his voice in total control. She could hear the disapproving tone to his voice.

Antonio looked relieved to see that she was all right, but she hesitated a moment before she answered. They stood an arm's length apart, not touching. Scanning his face, she realized how much she missed the way his eyes shone so brightly whenever they were together. She missed his touch and how excited she felt whenever he kissed her. Yet her mind told her to keep her guard up until she knew the truth.

She crossed her arms over her chest. "We have a lot to talk about," she said suspiciously.

"Yes, we do," he said in a low authoritative voice.

Rosemary walked past him and headed for the cafeteria. He followed her willingly. She found a table at a far corner of the room so they could be alone. He pressed his lips together, staring at her through narrow eyes, deciding how to ask her. Going back in time in his mind, the words *she doesn't want to see you any more* took control. She seemed cold to him as she sat on the opposite side of the table, one leg crossed over the other at the knee with her arms crossed in front of her and her eyes down. The scene of when they first met crossed his mind. She didn't even talk to him when he brought her home the first time. He decided to ask her exactly what was on his mind.

At the same time both of them started to talk.

"You first," Rosemary said in a bitter tone still looking at the table.

He cleared his throat. "Is it true? You don't want to see me anymore?" He asked, almost afraid to hear the answer.

His tone made her eyes shift to his face, which had turned cold and expressionless.

"Well, why didn't you tell me that you're one of Bugs Moran's boys?" She challenged. Antonio's face flashed red with anger as those words pierced his ears.

"Who told you that?" He asked gritting his teeth together.

He knew he had to control his temper, but he was getting more upset by the minute. His arms tensed up at his sides as his hands balled into fists.

"Does that matter?" She asked with an edge to her voice. Watching his reaction, she was afraid her dad was right. She saw how his muscles tensed beneath his shirt, and how his face grimaced with her words. She was afraid of his answer and how she would respond when she heard him say yes. She was in love with this man so would she actually end their relationship over that detail, or help him with his plan to leave the gang and move out of the country. She shuddered with the thought that her father was correct. Rosemary closed her eyes for a moment, feeling on the verge of tears. Then she took a careful breath.

"I want the truth. Do you work for Bugs Moran?"

She stared at him grimly, but Antonio knew she was not the enemy and he did not want to fight with her. His eyes traced the curve of her face and he thought of how much he missed her eyes. He took a deep breath and loosened his hands.

"Can you please tell me who told you that first?" He paused, "I am curious."

Rosemary hesitated a moment as she thought she heard a friendlier tone to his voice.

"My father," she said sarcastically, waiting to hear the truth.

"So, what did your father say exactly?" He asked flatly and folded his hands on the tabletop.

His body language came as a surprise to her. With the sudden calmness that he was now using, she inclined to lighten her tone. She could not make out what his next words would be. Was he or was he not in a gang with Bugs Moran?

"He said you were driving Bugs Moran around in his car the other day." She paused again and then added, "Well?" She searched his face for any kind of a clue to his guilt. She couldn't read it, but noticed that he wouldn't look her in the eyes after that statement. Maybe he was going to say the dreaded words she did not want to hear. She held her breath waiting for him to answer.

He looked forward past her face. "Is that all?"

"So he was right?" The words came tumbling out of her mouth with the exhale of her breath. She took her hands and wrapped her arms giving them a squeeze as she closed her eyes in disappointment. She could feel the tears welt up in the back of her eyes, so she tried not to show him. A single tear escaped rolling down her cheek.

"There is more to it than what you think," he whispered now beginning to understand what had happened. He never thought in a million years someone would see him drive that car, especially her father. Now to convince her that he was not in a gang.

"I don't understand?" Her voice cracked as she slowly opened her eyes and quickly swiped that lonely tear away.

"You know I work on cars with my father, right?" He stated still gazing past her.

She shook her head wishing his eyes would meet hers. She almost wished she hadn't of asked him, and they just kept up with their plans on leaving. She wished that she had not ignored him so that she would not have to feel her heart crushing as it was at this moment in time. Her throat had a large lump in it making it hard to swallow. She wished that she didn't know about Bugs and his involvement with Antonio. After all, Antonio was not like those other men. He was truthful, caring, and loving. A gangster was none of those things.

"We work sometimes on Mr. Moran's cars and he pays us very well," he continued. "The day your father saw me driving Mr. Moran around, I was taking a joyride in his beautiful Rolls Royce." He sighed as he went back in his memory of driving that beautiful car around town. "I couldn't resist the chance to sit behind the wheel."

He paused for a moment hiding his face in his hands. He wanted so bad to drive that car and never in his worse fears ever thought it would bring a wedge between him and Rosemary. Now he only wished that time would go back and he could refuse the offer to drive that car.

"If I would have known I would make enemies with your father, I would never have taken him up on his offer to get behind the wheel."

"Well are you are one of Moran's boys?" Her voice cracked.

He said nothing. Silence hung in the air.

"So you're not one of Moran's boys?" Her heart was on a roller coaster ride breaking one moment and beating the next. "Answer the question!"

He dropped his hands from his face and shook his head before answering. "You should know that answer, Rosemary," he sighed. "No."

What a relief to know that her father was wrong. With his answer, she felt her world coming around again. Everything made sense.

She thought for a moment, her eyes scanning his face. His eyes seemed gentle but intense, as he looked her way. Yes, deep down inside she knew there was no way this gentle man could be in any type of gang. Rosemary bit her lip as moisture formed in her eyes. *How could I ever have thought that he was a part of Moran's gang? How can I not believe his words?* She looked at him with glossy wet eyes and a slight smile on her face. She searched his face hoping he understood.

"My turn," he said with a frustrated tone. "Tell me why your father said you never wanted to see me again?"

"I don't know how," her voice quivered. "He's worried about me, that's all. Al..."

She hesitated dropping her eyes from his face. Her body started to shake and she needed to tell him, but how? She could feel perspiration take over her body as the words tried to get out.

"What?" he asked confused again. "You don't want to see me anymore?" He stretched his hand on the table and slowly moved it towards her. He didn't stop until he could touch her arm. She moved back and away from him making his hand fall back on the table. He drew his arm back to his side.

She closed her eyes only for a moment as she tried to come up with the right words. Unfortunately, there were no right words, so she just had to spit them out.

"Al Capone is my dad's cousin," she groaned and looked away from him. "It's dangerous for me to be seen with someone who hangs around with Moran when we are related to Al Capone." She glanced up and saw his expression was pained. *Did he hear me right?* She wondered.

He digested it in silence. Now this was making more sense to him. "Why didn't you tell me when I first met you?"

"I should have," she said. "But why would I tell you something that I am not proud of? I wanted to wait until I knew you better. . Or maybe not at all. . I was afraid that you would never want to go out with me again if you knew."

Antonio's heart pounded in his chest, as he imagined riding in a car with Rosemary sitting by his side and being seen by Capone. *He might kill me,* he thought.

"You realize that it is crazy for you and me to go out again." she said with an unreadable expression.

"I know," Antonio agreed. "Believe me I want to live to see tomorrow."

"What if I told you for our safety, I never want to see you again?"

He hesitated before he answered. His heart dropped with heaviness in his chest. "I guess I would leave you alone." He felt terrified of what was coming next. He needed from her soft words like a child needing a kiss to make it all better.

The comment hung in the air. Rosemary shifted in her seat. Her face winced. Did she really not want to see him again? Could she tell him goodbye? Her brain is screaming to walk away from him, while her heart is telling her to stay. In the grip of the silent panic her eyes dilate as her heart races. Her heart started to beat faster as her brain started to fire out negative thoughts, why she needs to leave him. The thoughts in her head were so fast and so disturbing that she felt like her heart was going to explode. She couldn't let it happen.

"You wouldn't even try to see me again at the coffee shop?"

Relief swept through Antonio when he heard those words. "Do you still love me, Rosemary?" He asked nervously as his eyes found hers. His brain tingled as a small smile tried to form on his lips.

Those words from him comforted her like a warm quilt on a cold winter day. "Yes," she answered without hesitating.

Antonio slowly rose from his seat and sat in the chair next to her. He put his arms around her and took in the sweet smell of the perfume from her hair. Tears rolled down Rosemary's cheeks as she held him tight. She snuggled her face in his chest and silently cried. A little voice inside her whispered that she needed to be careful, that nothing good could come of this, and she reminded herself that her father forbids her to have anything to do with Antonio. This was so confusing, but she also knew she was in love with him.

"What do we do now?" She sobbed.

Antonio let her go slowly and took her face in his hands. With his thumbs, he wiped her tears. Then drawing her face closer to his, he brushed her lips gently with his before answering.

"I don't understand the question," he whispered.

His breath was warm on her ear and made her shiver, as she got lost in the moment.

"My parents made me promise to not see you anymore," she gasped, afraid to perceive his face.

"Why?" He urged.

She thought about the conversation she overheard between Al and her father on how Moran went into a home to kill someone and the tone of Al's voice as he said he wanted revenge. The words she and Al shared on the porch also rung in her ears.

"Because they are afraid of Al," she continued. "I can't let my parents, or any of Capone's men, see us together." She paused for a moment to swallow. Her throat hurt from the tension she felt. "Al, himself, told me he saw you driving Bugs around."

Antonio felt her shiver.

"He told me to stay away from you."

He pressed his lips in a tight line. He had to think of a way to keep Rosemary safe and get them both out of this town. They sat in silence as they both pondered the situation. Antonio held Rosemary close. She closed her eyes as her head rested gently on his shoulder. A small smile formed on his lips as he took comfort in the fact that she still loved him. She was relieved to know that he had not lied to her and that he did not work for Bugs. Slowly, he put his hands on her shoulders and drew her away from him so he could gaze upon her face.

"Didn't you say you wanted to leave this town anyway?" He asked.

Rosemary looked up surprised. "Yes, I did," she replied without hesitation. Her eyebrows knitted close together while her nose scrounged up. *Where was he going with this?*

"Why don't we plan to leave soon?" he suggested. "I have some money saved and you said you would love to see Paris. . ."

The thought of leaving with him enticed Rosemary, but things had changed since her father forbade her to see Antonio. She would have to sneak away and not tell her parents. She was not afraid to leave, but would prefer not to do it like that. She had changed so much since she met Antonio. She was in love and yet she learned to be sneaky. She was not as open with her mother anymore. She was confused between the how she felt for her parents – their love and her obedience towards them, and how she felt about Antonio. She hated the fact she was related to Al and how complicated he made her life without even knowing it. Antonio saw her hesitation.

"No?" He asked, his face expressionless.

"I didn't say that," she said firmly. "It's just that I never thought I would have to lie to my parents and sneak out of town." Loyalty was never a question for her before.

Antonio gazed unrelentingly into her eyes. He understood the relationship she had with her parents and gently squeezed her shoulders.

"Rosemary, you could always leave them a note or write them a letter after we're gone," he whispered.

His breath on her ear made the hair on her arms rise. He then kissed her on the neck making goose bumps rise to her flesh.

As she gazed into his face, she noticed the clock on the wall behind him. Time had gotten away from them and she missed her classes. She really didn't care, but did need to be home on time so her parents wouldn't get suspicious.

"What is it?" He asked as he noticed her face grow tense.

"It's getting late. I can't be late getting home. You understand, don't you?" That would be all it took was one day home late and her parents would be suspicious. How was she supposed to love her parents and still be in love Antonio? Yet when he was by her side, all was well at that moment in time.

Antonio nodded as he moved her hair from her shoulder before helping her stand up. Pulling her close, he put his hand around her waist as they walked out of the cafeteria. She followed his lead wrapping her arm around him. Strolling with extra caution they made their way to the entrance of the school. He led her to the wall and leaned in toward her. Closing his eyes, he inhaled her scent one more time before he had to let her go. She put her arms around his waist and drew him near before kissing him goodbye. With one more kiss on her head, Antonio let her go and she walked toward the door.

"Oh, Rosemary?" He called after her with a faint smile on his lips.

"Yes?" she replied turning around letting her eyes meet his.

"Will I see you tomorrow?"

"I hope so," she said flashing smile, "but not at the coffee shop."

"The cafeteria," they said together.

In another part of town there was another meeting. Al sat in his chair, with his glass of bourbon watching the ice move in circles as he gently shook it. Tony sat across from him smoking a cigarette.

"Have you been following Rosemary around like I asked you to?"

"Yeah, boss, but there isn't much to tell. She is in school all day long."

"But is that boy with her?" His voice got a little louder. "I need to know if she is in trouble, or if Bugs is having her followed."

"I'm telling you; she is clean like a whistle. I watch her leave the house and walk to the bus stop. She sits on the bus and stays on it until her stop. Then she walks straight to school. Sometimes she is with a crowd of students, but none of them are any of Bugs men." He smiled to himself as he made a ring with the smoke.

"And when school is out?"

"Al, I have been sitting at her school the last three days. She doesn't leave the building until the end of the school day. Then she is usually walking with some of the other students straight to her bus." He tilted his head with his eyebrows down over his nose. "I don't think you have anything to worry about. Maybe she got smart and decided not to see him anymore."

"Mmm I hope you're right."

Chapter Twelve

A Plan to Kill Bugs

It was in his office in the Metropole Hotel where Al Capone held a meeting with his boys. The long, oblong table was littered with ashtrays, and half-drunk glasses of bourbon. Cigarette smoke hovered in the air above the men.

"It's time we make 'Bugs' pay for the murder of Patsy Lolordo," Al said as he took controlled steps around the table. His voice rung with authority. He was looking for answers.

All of his boys sat in their pin stripped suits smoking and listening to him intently. They included Frank Nitti, Jack 'Machine Gun' McGurn, and Tony 'Joe Batters' Accardo to name a few.

"Any ideas?" He threw out to them.

There was some mumbling going on, but no answers. Al sat down at the head of the table and took his time carefully looking around at each of their faces. The pain of losing his friend was making him impatient. His eyes were hard as he scanned at the men around him. He took his fist and hit the table hard. All the eyes around the table shot up at him.

"What's wrong with you, boys?" He shouted as his face turned red. "I want a contract out on Moran. How long will it take?"

He opened the pocket of his jacket, took out a cigar, and lit it while waiting for a response. Smoke circled his face before Jack from the other end of the table stood up.

"I have an idea," he said.

With the cigar hanging from his mouth Al replied, "On with it, boy. What do you have in mind?"

Jack stood up straight and tall before he answered. "Why don't we set a trap?"

Al's mouth formed a huge smile as he waved for him to join him. "Go on."

"Well, we could get a hijacker to contact Moran and tell him that we have a shipment of Old Log Cabin whiskey and that he will sell it to him at a very reasonable price per case," he explained as he walked slowly to the front of the table. All the eyes of the other boys watched him as he moved toward Al. "He could tell Moran that he wants to meet with him at the garage and when he shows up, we would be there to gun him down."

Al smiled, as he opened up his jacket. Taking out another cigar he waved the boy closer to him and gave it to him.

"I like this man," he said to the others at the table. "He's thinking. What's wrong with the rest of you? Why can't you think like that?"

"Jack," Al continued as he shook Jack's hand, "you will be in charge of this." He paused for a moment and then asked, "How long will this take to plan?"

"Give me about three or four weeks," Jack said smiling big showing all of his teeth.

"That's what I wanted to hear," laughed Al.

***

Hostilities between the North Side and the South Side gangs grew as the hatred between Bugs and Al festered making the City of Chicago a landmark for crime. The gangsters were becoming rich through their ownership of breweries, brothels, and gambling joints, but they wanted more. Chicago was becoming split between the two rival gangs. The illegal gambling operations increased, and the gangs continued to burglarize local stores and warehouses. Random shootings increased as gang members chased each other with the intent to kill and the politicians were still bought with election fraud.

The days went on and the streets remained dangerous, but Mike and Darlene had their store and their daughter, Rosemary. She came home safe from school every night and they were appreciative of Al for keeping their store safe as well. They came to Chicago for a good life and losing either one of them would be disastrous.

Antonio's name was never mentioned and it was as if he never existed, which hurt Rosemary. Dinners were still served and once in a while their cousin Al would join them. With laughter at the dinner table, disguising the true gangster he really was, Rosemary played the game of family with her cousin Al, even if she really didn't want to. And later in the evenings, Rosemary kept herself busy doing homework and studying.

Antonio also remained occupied taking on extra work to keep his mind off of things, but every night when he went to bed, he dreamed about his love, Rosemary. Of course, the two of them met regularly in the cafeteria where they shared a short hour of conversation, embraces, and even a few kisses.

Chapter Thirteen

Escape From Reality

One morning as Rosemary reached the school, Antonio's car sat in the parking lot by surprise. Smiling, she walked up and tapped on his window. With a mysterious smile, he rolled it down and she could see his eyes sparkle as he glanced up at her face.

"What are you doing here? It isn't lunch time yet. What if someone recognizes your car?"

"Come on inside for a moment," he said convincingly. "I want to ask you something." Without hesitation, she opened the passenger door and slid in.

"Hi," he said lovingly, gazing into her eyes.

She quickly closed the door never letting her eyes leave his.

"Hi," she said back as she crawled closer to him.

Antonio held her head in his hands and leaned inward to kiss her. She willingly molded into his kiss as her hands explored the back of his neck. Then slowly he pulled away, just far enough to stare into her eyes and still have her hands on his neck.

"I really need to see you again, Rosemary," he said giving her a couple of quick kisses on her lips.

She enjoyed the attention she got from him and realized how much she missed him.

"You are seeing me, silly," she giggled between kisses.

"I mean I want to go out somewhere with you again," he clarified shaking his head. "I want to lay my eyes on you someplace other than in the cafeteria."

Rosemary froze and her eyes grew large. He noticed the frightened expression on her face as her body stiffened.

"You'll be all right," he pleaded. "I'll be careful. I thought maybe we could go to the movies?"

A frown creased Rosemary's face as Antonio talked. He took her hands in his and held them tight, yet with love. His eyes explored her face with concern and hope.

"I thought maybe you could skip classes today so no one would know and you would still be home on time. And it is dark inside the movie theater so no one would recognize us."

Rosemary started shaking her head 'no.' She opened her mouth to speak, but nothing came out. She could feel a small pain start in her temple as she closed her eyes and took a deep breath. She wanted to see him to, but she was frightened to get caught. It would be bad enough for her parents to find out, but what if her cousin saw them? *Would he just take her by her hand and tell Antonio she is off limits, or would he gun him down in front of her?*

"I... I can't," she stuttered.

She tried to move away, but Antonio still had her hands in his. Her eyes skimmed to their hands before she peered up to his face.

"Please," he whispered.

She knew she could not deny him anything. He leaned in toward her ear and with a low voice he whispered, "I love you."

Goosebumps rose on her neck as his hot breath hit her skin. She was not real sure if they came because of his breath or because she was getting scared.

"We won't get caught," he added.

The conflict in her head would not give up. Yes, she wanted to go out with him outside of the school, but she did not want her parents to know she was still seeing him. She did not want to hurt them or lose their trust. His warm brown eyes dug deep into hers, which made him hard to resist. He leaned in one more time and kissed her neck. *He does not play fair,* she thought while enjoying his lips examining her throat.

"Fine," she said in defeat, "but please, let's not go anywhere someone might know us."

"Thanks," Antonio said before kissing her gently one more time.

She closed her eyes and enjoyed that kiss like it may be the last one he would ever give her. As his lips parted from hers, she watched his face as he moved away to drive. She noticed the way his lips turned up with a smile letting her know that he would always love her and keep her safe.

He put the car in gear, drove to Broadway Street and looked for the Uptown Theater. She could not believe how excited she was to go out with him again. All this time only meeting for a few minutes in a cafeteria made this trip even more exciting. The music was playing on the radio and they sang to the tunes being played. Once again, she felt like she was in back in heaven enjoying the man she loved. Neither of them brought up the fact she was related to Al or that he worked on Bugs car. This time was just for them alone to enjoy each other's company and not be afraid.

The main entrance of the theater was eight stories tall. Beautiful bronze chandeliers lit the main lobby with hand carved marble staircases, and individually hand sculpted gargoyles and griffins gave them a magnificent and regal appearance. Rosemary held tightly onto Antonio's hand as the uniformed usher led them down a plush red carpet to their seats. A red velvet curtain covered the huge movie screen and organ music could be heard. When the curtain finally rose, a movie called "The Cameraman" began.

Antonio sat close to Rosemary with his arm across her shoulders. They were about to be transported into a magical experience – at least for a little while. "The Cameraman" was a silent comedy about a photographer named Buster who had a secret crush on a secretary who works for MGM's newsreel department. He wanted to impress Sally so he got himself an old camera and tried to get a job as a cameraman. As luck would have it, the current cameraman also had a crush on her. Buster tried taking pictures and most of them were no good, but Sally seemed to like him anyway and accepted a date from him. As time went on, she also accepted a date with the other cameraman.

She was in a boat with him when an accident caused it to spiral out of control. The man saved himself, but not Sally. Buster happened to be out at the river at the same time taking pictures when he saw the accident and he jumped in to save her. Somehow, the other cameraman made Sally believe that he had saved her until a film was brought to their attention with the footage of what really happened. In the end, Buster and Sally walk off holding hands into the sunset together.

For a while, Antonio and Rosemary shared a different world, forgot their troubles, held each other tight and shared a few sweet kisses. She loved how it felt as he held her and missed him all over again. She went back in time to when he said to her, *'Don't you feel it?'* Now she knew what he was talking about. She was in love. Now she knew what her mother felt for her dad. But when that came to her mind, she hated the fact she could not share her happiness with them. She was not going to let that thought ruin this heavenly time for her. After all, she never knew she could feel so happy.

They had not been out in such a long time. Happy, holding hands, and smiling, they walked out of the theater. Their bodies close with fingers intertwined.

"This was a great idea, Antonio," she said as they swung their hands back and forth. "I should be getting home just in time and nobody will know the difference."

"I just had to be with you again, Rosemary. I miss you," he said. "Come on, I have something I want to show you."

"All right, but remember I have to be home in time." The trusting voice said.

They walked in step together down the boulevard toward the bridge that was over the Chicago River. The buildings that lined the street were so tall Rosemary had to lift her neck to see the tops. Listening to the cars whiz by and carefully crossing the street, they walked across the bridge. Some American flags were blowing in the wind and an occasional boat would honk as they floated down the river beneath them. It was cool and windy, and the sights and sounds made the city exciting and wonderful.

"Are you having fun?" Asked Antonio as he took his free hand and moved some hair from her face.

"Yes, this is wonderful," she squealed giving him a loving glance. The wind was strong and he helped her keep her balance as they stood at the end of the bridge taking in the city. *Who could believe that this beautiful city could be so corrupt?*

He could not help but bring her close and brush his lips against hers. She kissed him back with the assurance that all was well between them.

"Come on, we need to get you back home."

She let him take charge and followed his lead toward the car.

As they approached the car, he stopped and focused his eyes on her face as his lips drew near her mouth. Just as his lips brushed across hers, he heard the squealing of a car.

Antonio immediately spotted a car driving down the street and thought he recognized it. He had seen it before, but could not remember from where? He picked up his pace and pulled Rosemary along with him.

"Hey," she puffed trying to keep up. "Why are we walking so fast?"

Antonio didn't acknowledge her question. Instead he scanned the streets nervously. Up ahead he spotted another car moving slowly along the street and three men on the sidewalk strolling along with their hands at their pockets under their coats. Their hats shaded their eyes, which made them appear suspicious.

The thought of Rosemary being cousin to Al Capone's startled him at that moment. *Was he following them? Was he going to be killed just because he worked on George Moran's car? Or did Moran find out that he was dating Al Capone's cousin and wanted her dead?* Antonio turned the corner and pushed Rosemary toward the wall shielding her with his body. He quickly put his hand over her mouth while he watched to see what might happen next. Rosemary didn't try to move, but Antonio could feel her body tense up with fright.

"Shh," he whispered. "They didn't notice us."

The loud sound of metallic gunfire streamed from the car as it drove past the men. The horrific sound made Rosemary jump. She put her hand over his as she tried not to scream. Antonio placed his face next to her neck, shielding her. The repetition of the gunfire hurt her ears, but the thump of the men falling to the ground scared her even more. As they were hit, she heard their faint cries. Tears formed in her eyes as she stood hanging onto her bodyguard boyfriend. Then there was silence, except for the sound of the car speeding off. The men on the ground did not move. Antonio slowly let Rosemary go.

"I'm so sorry, Rosemary," he said giving her a hug. Not again she thought as her mind went back to the restaurant. Men killing men, she hated Chicago. *What if they did see them, would they also get hurt?* Her dream came back into her mind of her and Antonio having ice cream and Al killing him, saying stay away from her, she is family. She could not handle this anymore. She hated the killing, hated gang members, and her hatred for Al Capone was growing. *How much longer did she have to pretend to enjoy his company for the respect of her parents?*

His strong arms helped her walk her limp body to the car. He opened the passenger side door and aided her in. During the ride back to her school, they did not speak. The magical event of being together and enjoying each other's company came to an end. Her heaven just became hell all over again. *What if they had been shot and she never got to see her parents again, or even worse she would never get to see Antonio again?* She couldn't help herself as she wept with her hands covering her face. *Was this a sign telling her that she is never to see Antonio again? How could she even think that, since she was so much in love with this man?* This was also the second time he shielded her body willing to take a bullet for her. She did not want to go through this again. They had to make a choice.

"Last time we do this," she finally said breaking the silence. Her eyes peered up at his frightened face. She touched his hand before she continued. "We will meet from now on in the cafeteria."

Antonio let out a sigh of relief. He was so afraid that she was going to say that she never wanted to see him again. As he helped her out of the car, he pulled her to him. With his thumbs he wiped the tears from her face and then his lips met hers. "Until tomorrow, my love," he said looking deeply into her eyes.

"Yes," she said before she let him go. "I have to get home before mom gets suspicious." He nodded and kept his eyes on her until she got on her bus.

Chapter Fourteen

Secret Meetings

Rosemary could not be late coming home from school. Even though she assured her mother that she would be fine, her mom always waited by the front door, fearing for her daughter's life due to the random shootings. Rosemary also knew her father kept his eyes open just in case he spotted Antonio riding around in a car with Moran.

Rosemary also feared for Antonio's life. Al told her that he saw her boyfriend driving Bugs Moran around and to stay away from him. She knew Al would be on the lookout for her with Antonio. She knew they had to be extra careful and thinking back maybe that wasn't the best idea to go downtown the other day. She was immensely fearful that she might never see the man she loved again.

She looked forward to the noon hour each day – the only time they could see each other safely. And each day made it harder for them to be apart. Rosemary always saved a table by the wall so they could talk privately. She made it clear to Antonio that she loved her parents and she never wished to hurt them. She also helped him realize that she wanted to be with him forever – and in safety. For his part, Antonio said his love for her was the most important thing in his life and he would do anything to spend the rest of his life with her. They talked, held hands, and made plans for the future.

Since his nights were free, Antonio worked on extra cars to save enough money for their escape. He even fixed more cars for Moran, who paid well for his services. He knew that he might be putting himself in danger, but felt it was for a good cause. Antonio shared everything about himself with Rosemary, even about working on Moran's cars. Although that scared her, he asked her to trust him. She shared everything with him too. She let him know when Al came for dinner and how it hurt her to know her parents would not even say Antonio's name. Their time together always seemed short and all too soon, he had to kiss her goodbye.

One day at lunch, Rosemary put a tray with hot dogs and cokes on the table, and waited for Antonio. Her heart leapt as always when she spotted him walking into the room, but this time he threw her an anxious glance.

"I hate not being alone with you anymore," he said as he approached her. Antonio took her into his arms.

"I don't want to be without you either," she said looking into his eyes.

"I love you, you know," he said and leaned in to kiss her.

"I know," was all she could say before their lips touched.

He held her close and molded into the kiss more than he would usually do being in public. Slowly, he let her go and gazed back into her eyes.

"I miss you," he said as they sat down next to each other at the table. "Let's plan our getaway and leave soon."

"What do you have in mind?" She asked taking his hand in hers.

He lightly traced the shape of her lips with his fingers and she trembled.

"How about a romantic get away," he whispered in her ear.

Chills ran up and down her body as she felt his breath – the same familiar feeling that she missed so much. She didn't give herself anytime to think she just asked, "When?"

He leaned down and kissed her neck. "Valentine's Day."

He took her face in his hands and kissed her deeply with unyielding lips moving against hers. Her arms reached around his neck and she held him tightly.

"How?" She gasped as he slowly let her go. Her heart was thumping in her chest so fast she was having trouble catching her breath.

He clasped her hand firmly. "We can go to Paris," he said. "I will figure out the way. I can't come to your place but you can meet me at the coffee house at 2100 North Clark Street." He paused for a moment hoping she wanted the same thing. "I can pick you up and we'll leave together to start our new life."

His eyes penetrated hers waiting for an answer. Rosemary's lips formed a small curve as she scanned his face. Her mind swiftly traveled to her parents and how she would tell them goodbye. But just as fast, her mind – and heart – returned to Antonio.

"Okay," she agreed not letting her eyes leave his. *This is exactly what I want – to go away with him,* she thought. *Then we will finally be together.*

"This will be my Valentine's Day gift to you," he continued, "the start of a new life for you and me."

As always, the hour flew by while they ate and talked. Reluctantly, she walked with him to the front door of the school and gave him one last kiss before watching him leave. The rest of the day, she could barely concentrate as she pondered the trip they had planned. She tried to see herself telling her parents goodbye, but none of the visions seemed just right. She was a little torn leaving with maybe only a letter, but then Antonio would come back into her head, the way he looked at her, touching her, telling her that he loved her and all would be right in the world again. She told herself she would figure it out closer to the day and not to worry about that now. Her excitement stayed with her even as the school day ended.

"Hey, Ma," she shouted bounding in the front door.

She walked into the kitchen to find potatoes, carrots, and celery on the table. Her mother was sitting by the table busy peeling the skins off the potatoes. When she heard her daughter come in, she glanced up.

"Hi, child," she said. "Do you want to help?"

"Sure," Rosemary replied walking next to her mother and planting a kiss on her cheek.

"I need the carrots and celery cut up for the pot roast."

Rosemary grabbed an apron out of the drawer and tied it around her waist. She felt she should spend as much time as possible with her mother. It would not be long before she left and might never see her again. She took in her mother's face and the pair of eyes that mimicked hers. She watched how fast and gracefully her mother pealed the potatoes knowing that she would miss all this.

"So how was school today?" Her mother asked. "Did you have any tests today?"

"Nope, not today," she answered in an animated voice.

Rosemary blushed as she thought of Antonio and how she was secretly seeing him. She hoped her mother didn't notice. Darlene finished peeling the potatoes and started to cut them. When Rosemary finished cutting the carrots and celery, she helped her mom cut up the rest of the potatoes. She watched her mother as she grabbed two towels and carefully opened the oven. She pulled out a rack with the pot roast on it and took off the cover. Picking up the platter she slid in the vegetables. The kitchen smelled so good.

"You outdid yourself again, Ma," Rosemary said taking in a big whiff.

"You need to cook with me more often. Remember what I told you?" She asked with a giggle.

"The way to a man's heart," Rosemary joined in, "is through his stomach." Rosemary put on a fake smile and hugged her mother. "I know, Mama," she said sadly as she sat on the chair and pulled up her legs hugging her knees.

The thought of leaving with Antonio all of a sudden haunted her mind. She did not want to leave her family. She went back in time when all four of them sat around the table talking and laughing. *Why did everything have to change?* She wondered.

"You miss him, don't you," her mother unexpectedly said.

Rosemary flashed her eyes up in surprise.

"I was your age once, child. I remember what my first love felt like."

Her mother sat down at the table, placed an elbow on it, and put her head on her hand. She closed her eyes as if envisioning something from the past. Then she focused intently on Rosemary.

"Are you still seeing him?" She asked sternly changing her mood.

Rosemary did not like to lie so she offered no response. Her mother's continued stare caused her to squirm.

"It's very dangerous, Rosemary. You know that. You could get killed if you were to get caught with him."

"Ma," she replied without thinking, "he's not a part of Moran's gang." Realizing what she just said, she put her hand over her mouth.

"You have been seeing him," her mother said, disappointment coloring her face. "You promised you would not see him anymore... I can't trust you?"

Rosemary got off her chair and moved in front of her mother bending down on her knees. She took her mom's hands in hers as she peered into her eyes. She had to find a way to make her mother understand.

"Ma, I love him. You understand, don't you?"

"But your father warned you... and Al is your dad's cousin."

Rosemary could see the tears welling in her mother's eyes. What could she say or do to ease her mother's mind?

"Ma, dad was your first love, wasn't he?"

"I'm so afraid for you, Rosemary," she said blinking the tears onto her cheeks.

"Mom, he is not one of Moran's boys," she repeated as her own tears began to flow. She brought her mother's hands to her lips and gave them a kiss before she went on. "He's only a mechanic and sometimes Moran brings his car in to get worked on." She could feel her mother's body shaking. "He is not part of Bugs Moran's gang, mom," she said hopefully reassuring her.

Darlene withdrew her hands and wrapped them around Rosemary's head as if to hug her. Then she kissed the top of her head before she let her go.

"What about the part of your young man driving Mr. Moran around?" The words got stuck in her throat as she spoke them.

"He just finished fixing his car and Mr. Moran offered to let him drive the car." She felt her mother's body shake. "Honest, ma, that is all it was. He does not work for that man and is not a gangster."

"So you believe what he told you?"

"Yes, ma, with all my heart." Rosemary thought she felt her mother's body relax a little. "Please believe me, ma. I am in love, but not with a gangster." She raised her head and kissed her mother on the cheek. "Please don't tell dad," Rosemary said with pleading eyes.

Darlene shook her head and a few more tears escaped down her cheeks. "I love you, Rosemary."

"I love you too, Ma."

The next couple of weeks passed slowly as Rosemary and Antonio planned their trip with the little time they could spend together in the cafeteria. Rosemary helped her mother around the kitchen more often, knowing she would soon be gone. But she had to be careful. She had told her mother that she was still seeing Antonio, but she did not mention their plan to leave together. Antonio worked harder than ever taking on extra jobs so he would have money for them to live on. Their love grew with the anticipation of where their future might lead, tangled with thoughts of the exciting trip ahead.

Chapter Fifteen

Gangland Revenge

A few days before Valentine's Day, Jack 'Machine Gun' McGurn, one of Al Capone's men, held a meeting with some of the boys at the Circus Café. The lighting was dim and cigarette smoke hung in the air. As he strolled into the café, he saw a few couples sitting at tables with drinks in their hands. The muffled beats of music thumped through the place. Women hung around the bar eyeing any young man who might be lonely and seeking companionship. As Jack walked toward the back of the building, women asked him to light their cigarettes and inquired if he wanted any company. He waded his way through them and when he entered the meeting room, he saw that he was the last to arrive. The men stood around smoking, drinking and talking waiting patiently for him to arrive.

"Hello, boys," he said spreading a map of the neighborhood across the pool table. "This is it. What we all have been waiting for."

All of the boys gathered around him.

"A car will be hiding here," he said marking the map with his finger.

His plan was that a stolen police car would be stored in a nearby garage. When he looked up, he glanced at four men standing near the back of the room that were unknown to the rest of the group.

"Okay, then what?" Asked one of the gangsters.

"We have to be careful that Moran, or any of his men, don't recognize us. Let me introduce you to Fred Burke, John Scalise, Albert Anselmi, and Joseph Lolordo, part of the Mafia," he said walking toward them. "Thanks for coming." He shook each of their hands. "They're going to pull the trigger when Moran goes to the garage for the whiskey. Moran won't recognize them, so he'll have no idea that they're with us."

Each of the men took turns saying hello as they shook hands with the men before walking back to the pool table following Jack.

"We found Moran's headquarters in this large garage behind the offices of S.M.C. Cartage Company," he noted getting their attention back. "We're going to have a bootlegger lure Moran into his garage to buy some very good whiskey."

"Are you sure he'll show up alone?" Asked one of the men.

"Good question," Jack said. "We found an Italian bootlegger who hijacked some of Moran's whiskey a week ago. We'll have him call Moran with another load. His story will be that he doesn't like the way his boys treated him and will only deal with Moran by himself."

A few low grumbles filled the room.

"Hold on," Jack continued. "I know what you're thinking. Why would Moran do this himself?"

A lot of heads nodded and many replied, "Yeah."

"He's going to sell the whiskey for $57 per case, only if Moran arrives to make the deal personally," he continued shaking his head. A big smile appeared on his face as he continued. "He will take the deal. It's a darn good price if you ask me... Here," he noted pointing to the map again, "is where the lookout apartment will be." He looked around the room. "Harry and Phil?" He shouted looking their way. "You will be responsible for watching for Moran and telling us when he arrives at the garage."

No one spoke as they looked at the map and Jack's markings of lines and directions. Then he pulled out a picture of Moran.

"He usually wears a tan overcoat," he said moving toward the Keywell brothers, "so you should notice him really easy. Any questions?" He asked turning around.

"Do you think he will come alone?" Yelled one of the men.

"I don't really know, but will it matter?" Laughed Jack.

"Yeah, I have one," called out a voice from the back of the room.

Everyone turned to find the voice.

"When are we going to do this?"

Jack donned a huge grin before answering, "Valentine's Day!"

Chapter Sixteen

Get Away Plans

Rosemary and Antonio were busy making plans for their getaway. It was snowing outside, leaving the bare trees with a new dust of white color. The cold wind hit Antonio in the face, but his neck was warm with the scarf he wore. He left foot prints from his car up the steps and before he went into the school, but he knew they would be covered up again with the newly fallen flakes. They had to be careful. It was the day before Valentine's; they met in the cafeteria as usual.

Rosemary eagerly waited at a table with two cokes, two hamburgers, and fries to share. Guilt sat not in her chest but in her brain. She never tried to deceive her parents before. She prayed that one day she would feel removed from this sin, washed clean of it. Anticipation was in the air and her heart leapt when she saw the outline of Antonio's body come through the door. He was late but that didn't matter. *Why waste the little time we have together worrying about such minor things?* She thought.

"Hi," he said and leaned in to kiss her forehead. He closed his eyes, sucked in her sweet perfume, and smiled. Then he took a seat across from her.

"Hi," she responded. "You're late!" She added folding her arms across her chest and feigning distress. She quickly forgot that she didn't want to bring that up.

"Is any of that for me?" He asked teasingly as he noticed the tray of food.

Quickly, Rosemary stood up to place a coke and burger in front of him. She waited for him to take a bite before she took her seat and picked up her burger.

"You aren't having second thoughts, are you?" He asked as he ran his hand through his hair. He studied her face trying to read it. Antonio wanted the happy version of Rosemary. The one with the instant smile and warm things to say. He didn't want her sad. This was a big decision and the day was finally around that would change their life forever.

For the first time she thought she saw a flash of impatience cross his features, and then just as fast it was gone.

"What's wrong?"

He could feel the fear in his chest trying to take over. "I'm asking will you be mad at me a year from now, saying that I made you do something you didn't want to do?" He paused as if looking for the right words as anxiety grabbed him by the tongue. "You are doing something so totally different for you. You have agreed to run away with me. And I am afraid you will have regrets, that you will learn to hate me." His body was tense while his eyes looked for clues on how she felt

Rosemary's eyebrows knit together and she looked at him curiously. She knew she would miss her parents, especially her mother, but she had convinced herself that it would not be forever. In time, she hoped she would be able to come back home again. You can have happiness and excitement but what if you didn't feel hurt or pain? The trick was to balance the good with the bad. She told herself everything would be alright. Fear can only hold her back from reaching her dreams. She loved Antonio and this was going to be a victory to be with the man she loves.

"No," she replied shaking her head, her eyes glued to his face. "You?"

"Of course not!" Antonio spoke with a steady voice as his body relaxed.

Rosemary reached over and touched his hand. He took her hand and squeezed it.

"How are you going to sneak out of the house?" He asked, squinting his eyes making lines across his forehead.

She took her hand back and took another bite of her burger before she answered. "I don't have to sneak out. Mom and dad usually leave for work before I go to school. I'll wait until they're gone before I pack."

Antonio's face smoothed as he heard her speak with no hesitation in her voice.

Antonio knew he would miss his father and siblings, and he realized that it might hurt his father if he left unexpectedly. However, his dad was the one who had told him that he eloped to be with his mother. It was something that he too had to do if he wanted to have a life with Rosemary.

He turned to Rosemary and replied, "I want to be with you forever. You know that... don't you?" He peered deeply into her eyes and fell in love with her all over again. Then he rose from his chair and took a seat beside her. "You mentioned where we would meet," he said putting an arm around her shoulders. "Where was it again?"

Rosemary let her cheek fall next to his face, closed her eyes, and whispered, "At the coffee shop... 2100 North Clark Street."

She hugged his waist and wished that lunchtime was not over yet. She would have to go back to class and miss him for yet another night.

"No second thoughts!" Antonio reaffirmed and kissed her cheek.

"Right," she replied turning her face toward his.

Then his lips found hers one last time before they parted.

Chapter Seventeen

Valentine's Day

Rosemary arose that morning and checked outside her bedroom door to make sure her parents had left for work. She pulled out a suitcase she had hidden under the bed and quickly started to pack. After an inviting bubble bath, she put on her slip and pinned her long black hair up in a French twist. Her heart pounded as thoughts of Antonio and their trip played out in her mind. *No Second thoughts,* she remembered telling him. Finally, their dream was going to come true. They would be with each other forever and live somewhere, where the violence was not rapid in the city like it was here in Chicago.

Glancing around the room, she scanned all of the familiar things that had played an important part in her life in the past, like the curtains she proudly sewed herself and the ribbons she won over the years from spelling bees. Although she had not even left yet, she felt the pangs of homesickness. Glancing at her dresser, she realized that she almost forgot to take the picture of her with her parents. She opened her suitcase and carefully placed the frame inside some clothing, wrapping it to keep it from breaking.

As she walked down the stairs, she could smell bleach and instinctively knew that her mother must have just cleaned the kitchen. She glanced into the dining room, looked at the china cabinet that held so many family memories, and then strolled into the living room. She gazed upon her dad's favorite chair trying to picture him relaxing in it. Before opening the front door, she hesitated. Sadness hit her for a moment as she swallowed down the bitter pill knowing that later she would be with Antonio and all would be well again.

I might never come home again, she thought sadly.

Outside, the cold Chicago weather made hailing a cab an inviting idea. After exchanging polite gestures with the cab driver, she silently rode with anticipation in her heart for her journey ahead.

***

Antonio awoke when he heard the telephone ring. He jumped out of bed to eavesdrop on his father. He was agreeing to take on another job that morning for Bugs. Antonio quickly ran to his father's side.

"Who was that?" He asked trying not to sound too excited. In the back of his mind, the thought of making extra money sounded good. He was living at this time for a mission to seek a new life with his love Rosemary and every little bit count.

"It was George," his dad replied as he walked into the kitchen. Picking up the pot and filling it with water, he put in the coffee grounds to make his coffee. Antonio pulled out a kitchen chair and sat down. His hair ruffled and a slight growth of hair on his face as he yawned.

"Well, what did he want?"

"He needs me to replace a transmission this morning on one of his cars – a rush job at the garage."

"Can I do it?" The words rushed out of Antonio's mouth.

He thought about Rosemary waiting for him. However, he figured she would understand if he was late. Bugs paid good money and every little bit would help. He knew he would need to find a job once they left town, but until then he wanted to make sure they had enough to live on. It was still early, just 8 a.m. He figured the job should not take him more than a couple of hours.

"I'll think about it, son," John said between yawns. "But it is in his garage, not ours, and some of his crew might be there. . . . But I will think about it."

"Thanks, Dad."

***

It was a frigid morning when John received the call. He was told that if he replaced the transmission on Bugs' car immediately, he would make an extra $20. Needing the money, John agreed. He was one of the first men to reach the garage. Bugs had called the Gusenberg brothers, Frank and Pete, to help with the load of whisky. Albert Weinshank, James Clark, and Adam Heyer showed up as well.

Meanwhile, Harry and Phil Keywell kept a look out from the apartment across the street as Bugs' boys walked into the building. They still had not seen Bugs. Waiting impatiently, Harry noticed a man with a tan coat enter the building and thought that might be him. He told Phil to call the crews waiting at the Circus Café so they could begin their fake raid. Phil ran along the hallway to a pay phone and made the important call that they hoped would lead to Bugs' death.

In a different garage Fred, John, Albert, and Joseph anxiously awaited. Two of them were dressed as police officers and the other two wore long trench coats. They were excited when they got the call. Yep, Moran was noted being seen walking into the garage. Quickly, they drove to the garage in the stolen car. Creeping quietly, they went inside through the offices. Peering through the window of the doors, they observed six of Bugs' men and the man in the tan coat whom was to be Moran. Joseph nodded to the others and the two dressed like police officers busted in the garage while the other two waited behind the door.

"Line up, boys!" Hollered one of the fake officers.

John got wind of the commotion and told Antonio to hide under the back seat of the car. Antonio couldn't believe his ears as he obeyed his father. He was actually in the middle of a raid. This made him become more anxious to get Rosemary out of this city.

"You've got to be kidding?" Adam said with an aggravated expression. His face glowered at the expressionless face that told him to move. He grabbed some money out of his pocket and tried to pass it to one of the officers as he was being told to go to the wall.

"Get over there," the officer yelled as he threw the money on the floor.

He pushed Adam toward the wall, a move that angered him. The officers did not talk to each other, only yelled orders at the men.

"Hey, watch the material," Pete barked. He balled his hand into a fist and pushed the officer back. "Do you know who we are?"

"I don't recognize any of you cops," yelled Albert. "I am not sure you know who you are dealing with here." He shrugged the hand that was holding his shoulder off him.

"Someone's going to hear about this," Frank said angrily shaking an arm off his sleeve.

All of the men were herded to the back wall. Having respect for the men in blue, they co-operated and did as they were told. With a quick glance at the car sitting inside, one of the officers could not help noticing that someone was working on it. He rushed over to the vehicle.

"All of you, by the wall," he said jerking John up by the back of his shirt.

"Hey, I'm only the mechanic," John said frightened as a pair of rough hands pushed him between the gangsters. "Now face the wall. All of you."

The two police officers started to frisk the men taking away any hardware they carried, which made them even more upset. However, they let them take their guns without a fight, thinking this was a raid – but words did fly. The seven men then stood defenseless, with no weapons. One of the officers opened the door to let in the other two gangsters. Standing directly behind the seven men – one pointing to the left, one to the right, and two to the middle – they started shooting. Using two Thompsons – one with a 20-round clip and one with a 50-round clip – and two shotguns, they let loose on the men right in their backs.

It sounded like thunder when the bullets hit their bodies and slammed into the brick wall. Then there was a metallic sound as the bullets hit the water pipes. All of the downed men shook with the beat of the bullets until they finally hit the floor. They were riddled with holes over their bodies and their blood sprayed onto the wall dripping to the floor. Pieces of the brick flew into the air as the bullets hit. Chairs fell to their sides. They did not stop shooting until they used all of their ammunition. Surveying the damage, they saw the men lying still with bullets to their heads, backs, arms, and legs – each one in a pool of blood.

Tears filled Antonio's eyes as he huddled silently in the backseat of the car. Hearing the metal ricochet and the men cry out in agony was more than he could bear. He put his hands over his mouth so they would not hear his heavy gasps.

Hiding their weapons, the two gangsters dressed as police officers walked out of the building behind the two dressed in trench coats with guns to their backs. They left with their hands in the air like they were being arrested, but then they all jumped into the stolen vehicle and sped away.

Through the café window Rosemary watched the caper go down. From the garage across the street, two men exited with the bull quick on their heels. She tried to focus on them without being noticed. She was not sure if she recognized any of them. All four of them entered a Cadillac sedan and sped away. She did not see blood or any bodies lying on the ground thankfully. Knots formed in the pit of her stomach. She felt like something was wrong. In her heart she knew she had to investigate further. As the car sped away, the loud chatter of different ideas of what may have happened filled the coffee shop. The crowd dispersed back to their seats.

Rosemary left her chilled coffee on the café table with a small tip and exited. No sooner than she let the door slip, someone wearing a tan overcoat and hat bumped into her. She heard whoever is was mumble an apology before they disappeared inside. She hesitated for just a small moment; with the idea she knew who this man was. She felt an uncomfortable sensation run through her body when he bumped into her. *Maybe she recognized him? Could that be Mr. Moran?* But the fleeting thought left her just as fast as she ran toward the garage. Fighting the wind took her breath away and sent a new chill through her body. When she reached the door, she hesitated for a moment before touching the knob. It seemed like slow motion as she turned her hand and opened the door. She waited for only a moment to listen, but the only sound was her footsteps as she stepped with one foot deliberately in front of the other past the offices at the front of the building. Taking a deep breath first, she reluctantly opened the door to the garage. It made an eerie creaking sound as it exposed what was behind it. Without warning, a gasp escaped her lips as she stumbled upon a horrible scene. Her hand slapped across her mouth trying to contain any kind of fear she may let out. She had heard stories about things like this, but she could never have imagined them happening in real life.

Tears filled her eyes as she tried to focus on the bloody sight before her. The brick wall was sprayed red. Blood slowly dripped to the floor where seven men lay dead; their bodies riddled with bullet holes. She stood memorized by the horrific sight in front of her. Then fear took over her body and she stiffened, afraid to move. Hearing tales of such violence was incomparable. Standing there it seemed as if the blood was slowly seeping toward the door. *Was she hallucinating?* One of the bodies attempted to crawl to the door through the bloody mess. He stopped and squinted up at her before he called her by name.

"Rosemary... get out of here... now," he labored to say in his weakened state.

Frightened beyond belief, she ran to his side. He was badly hurt and trying to crawl to the door. She did not recognize him with all the blood, but she knew his voice. Tears streaked her once excited face.

"John?" She whispered. "Is that you? Where is Antonio?"

He tried to point to the left side of the garage.

"Who did this?" She asked in a halting voice.

He glanced up at her and with his last breath said, "Capone."

"John," she yelled, but he didn't move.

Without haste, she ran out of the garage devastated, confused, and angry. Her body shook so badly that she had to hold onto a wall or she would have fallen. She gasped for air and tried to calm down. Her hands were frozen from the cold while her tears frosted on her face. She held an arm firmly across her stomach and made her way back inside the garage. As she did so, she heard the distinct squeal of sirens in the distance.

I have to go back in there, she thought. *I have to find Antonio.*

She found the door to the garage again and made herself open the latch. As she viewed the devastating sight one more time, she knew she must find him and prayed that he was still alive. She spotted a car sitting inside with the engine open.

John must have been working on that one, she thought.

Tip toeing around the vehicle, she saw a couple of bullet holes by the back door. Her eyes brought her to a trail of blood leading away from the car, but it did not lead toward the brick wall. She followed the trail to a different door leading out to the alley. By that time, she heard people rustling inside and the sirens grew louder. She opened the door, walked outside, and quietly closed it behind her – still following the path of blood. It appeared as if someone had dragged themselves out of the building.

She crept slowly until her fear became reality and she saw Antonio lying in the snow. She studied him briefly, the front of his clothes was torn and a couple of bullet holes left his abdomen gaping with blood all around him.

"Antonio!" She screamed. Her legs seemed stagnant and would not move. She could see his body lying there with no life.

"Please, Antonio," she said calling to him as loud as she could.

Slowly, his lashes fluttered as he tried to focus on the voice that called his name. With every ounce of strength, Rosemary dashed to his side. Her knees hit the snow while her hands stopped her from sliding, before she sat down by his body and gently picked up his head and laid it on her lap. The ground was icy cold, but she could not feel it. She scanned his frame and gasped at the bright red blood running away from his body making its own path in the once pure white snow. Taking her fingers, she moved the hair off his forehead before she brought her face down toward his and kissed his forehead over and over again.

This cannot be happening, she thought. *They were supposed to leave today and go far far away from this wretched city and live happily ever after. They made plans. They were even willing to leave their families without a notice so they could be together. How was she supposed to live without him now?* Memories of his body shielding hers from flying bullets only to save her life and he hardly even knew her, the hungry moment when he held her tight and their lips first touched on the dance floor, when he acted so different asking her if she feels it to, letting her know how much he loved her... She needed to try and save him now.

In the distance sounds of people rushing into the warehouse and more sirens blaring down the street could be heard, while peaceful white snowflakes started to fall. She looked up to see only a white sky that drifted down to earth. It should be beautiful, but now it felt lonely and cold.

"Don't leave me, Antonio," she cried kissing his cheeks in despair.

He managed to gaze up at her with loving eyes. He exhaled which she thought was a good sign. She brushed her lips to his, while big alligator tears ran down her face. *Be strong,* she told herself. *Don't let him know how bad he is hurt.*

"Help!" She yelled, her breathing hard and fast. She held him close, and rocked him back and forth as she gulped for breath. She never felt so frightened in her life. "Please help me!" Her voice echoed through the narrow alley as she scanned the area around them for anyone who would hear her.

"Rosemary?" A faint voice asked.

She immediately recalled the first time he said her name a year ago at the coffee shop with such a musical tone. He held a flame for her before she even knew who he was. He loved her and he was the best thing that ever happened to her.   Letting her eyes search his face, she took two fingers and brushed his cheek before lightly covering his mouth.

"Don't talk now, my love," she said trying to use a fearless voice, trying to act brave. "I'll find you some help." She paused and noticed the blood getting thicker on the ground.   "Everything will be fine," she soothed, but her voice trembled.

Then she heard someone yell back to her. She folded her fingers and thumb around her lips like a cup and screamed, "Over here!" as loud as she could.

"I love you," Antonio whispered as he attempted to pick up his hand to reach her shoulder. A glimpse of a smile formed on his lips. His fingers lightly touched her shoulder.

"I love you too," she cried gazing deeply into his eyes. "You know you are the best thing that ever happened to me. You make me feel alive and I want you to know that you are the very best part of me."

Taking his fingers to her lips she kissed his knuckles. Time stood still, just for a moment until his arm dropped and his eyes closed.

"No, Antonio! Come back!" She sobbed. She leaned down and kissed him on the lips. Then she took him in her arms and held him tight. She knew this would be the last time she would ever hold him again. She stayed that way for a while. The snow began to fall faster now, but she didn't notice. She took a long, slow breath and when she finally spoke her voice sounded distant. "I will never forget you, Antonio."

She struggled to make her way back home. Her dream was gone. Her love was dead. The snow was falling making it harder to walk without slipping. She skidded and fell. She picked herself up for a short distance, before she lost her footing and glided back down again. Somehow, she made her way back home. Some people asked her if she was all right and some people asked her if she wanted any help. She didn't talk to anyone. Rosemary walked and walked until she made it to her house.

Later that night she sat in her living room with a closed suitcase and mascara running down her face. Her once neatly pinned up hair had strands falling down around her shoulder. Her off white jacket was covered in blood. Her mother and father walked into the house talking about their day, until they saw her. Darlene stopped and froze in her tracks.

"My dear," she said, her voice shaking, afraid to move. "What is this, what happened?"

Mike stared in disbelief, not really sure of what he was seeing. He blinked repeatedly to clear his vision. He pressed his lips together in a tight line.

Rosemary was stoic. She didn't say a word, her skin white and cold.

Darlene rushed to her side. "Are you hurt?" she asked, with fear in her voice, kneeling in front of her daughter.

Rosemary shook her head no, showing no expression or emotion. Darlene touched her daughters face. "You are so cold?" She got up to find an afghan.

"Whose blood is this?" She asked as she placed the blanket around her daughter's shoulders.

Mike walked around the room, with his hands in fists. He started rambling in Italian.

"Remember your blood pressure," said Darlene watching her husband pace.

Mike's face got red and he finally stopped walking in front of his daughter. "You are seeing that boy again, aren't you?" He demanded. "He did this to you."

Rosemary's face shot up and her eyes glared at her father. Her eyes were cold and lips drawn in a line. She could not take anymore, and slowly stood up to face her father. The afghan fell off her shoulders and onto the couch. Her mother stood up and walked backwards in total horror at the scene before her.

She gathered up all her strength. "See this blood," she screamed, her eyebrows turned down to her nose, "Your cousin did this." Her hands flapped back and forth to the blood on her jacket and swung out in the air and back again to her jacket. "The man you always have over for dinner. The man you call family."

Darlene trembled watching her daughter. "Wh-Whose blood is that?" She stuttered.

"ANTONIO'S!" Rosemary shouted. "And Al is responsible for his death!"

Mike kept his ground. "How can that be, Rosemary?" her dad hollered. "He is in Florida."

"Florida?" Darlene's surprised voice asked as her head went back and forth watching the two of them talk. "When did he go there?"

"I don't know. I guess a couple of days ago. But I know for a fact he was not here and did not kill your Antonio."

Rosemary turned her face with an evil eye. "Yes he did, father. One of the men in the garage was still alive when I got there. Maybe he did not physically kill him, but he planned this massacre that killed all those men."

"You were at the garage where seven men got executed this morning?" He said interrupting her.

"Yes ... I ... Was." She said using one word at a time with a defiant tone. "I had plans to run away with Antonio. He was going to take me to France and get out of this evil gangster town."

Mike stood with his mouth open, no words coming out. He turned his face towards his wife. She stood there with her face in her hands crying. He slowly walked to his chair and slumped down.

"Any way," the angry voice carried on, "the man told me it was the work of Al Capone. And he will pay for taking my love from me."

Finally exhausted by anguish and pain, she fell back onto the couch and the tears began to fall. Her body shook uncontrollably as she gasped for breath between the sobs. Darlene rushed to her child and slid the afghan back on her shoulders. She sat next to her bringing Rosemary into her arms, rocking her back and forth. Mike got up and paced around the room with his hands behind his back taking this all in.

"We need to talk, Rosemary," his stern but quiet voice said. Watching his daughter in such distress was more than he could handle.

"She needs a shower and some food and rest," interrupted Darlene with a demanding voice.

Rosemary glanced up at her father.

"I moved here for a better life," he began to say. "I already lived through the killing of my parents because of Al. Don't get me wrong, he didn't kill them, but they were killed because he was a part of our family."

Rosemary took in a deep breath making her body shake as she listened. Her eyes were tired and her vision was doubled.

"I don't believe in violence," he stated. "I am not sure about Antonio, if he worked for Bugs Moran or not."

"No, he was not working for Bugs," the troubled crackling voice interrupted. "But say he did, would that be a way to kill a man?"

"No," his voice squeaked.

"Papa," she said in a weak voice. "I was in love with this man. He only worked on Moran's cars. He didn't even own a gun. He was not a gangster." Memories rushed into her head, the way he said her name like it was music, and his touch was so electric making her feel so alive and on fire. She still couldn't comprehend that she was never going to see him again.

"Then you will understand that when you said the words, *he will pay*, I hope you didn't mean to kill. . . That will make you the same kind of person as Bugs Moran and your cousin Al."

She sucked in another big breath as her head bobbed up and down.

"I know you are upset and you feel like your whole world just came to an end, but your life is still ahead of you." He paused and sighed out loud.

"Listen to your mother, you need to take a shower and get some food in your stomach. Who knows when the last time you ate?" His eyes took in her face. "In the morning you can go to the authorities and tell them what you know. Revenge will only harm you, but doing this the right way you can make his death be for something good. We can honor Antonio's death with the thought that he helped put a stop to all this hatred."

"T-T-That is all he wanted," she stuttered. "He wanted to take me away from the violence in this town where we could live happy and not be afraid to walk the streets at night."

Mike crossed the room toward his daughter and taking her arms he helped her stand up, before he pulled her close and wrapped his arms around her. Kissing her on the head, he whispered, "I'm sorry for your loss."

Darlene came to the other side of Rosemary and hugged her making a sandwich out of her between them.

"If this was truly the handy work of my cousin, he finally crossed the line and even I can't help him now."

NEVER GIVE UP ON SOMEONE YOU CAN'T LIVE A DAY WITHOUT

Made in the USA
Middletown, DE
26 January 2022